COME and get your GLOVE

Come and Get Your Glove

© copyright 2025 J.P. Sterling

Editors: Rebecca Carpenter and Perfect Pages Editor

CONTENTS

To Kaci.

Thank you for always being the sweetest and supportive person you are.

I hope you enjoy your book.

BLURB

ALL NEW SWEET HOCKEY ROMCOM Goalie + Single Mom + Forced Close Proximity

Come and Get your Glove

Sometimes opposites really do attract—even when you are skating in the wrong direction.

Being a single mom juggling work, college, and life is already enough to keep me on my toes. The last thing I need—way down at the bottom of my never-bucket list—is getting tangled up in a series of bizarre events that links me to Granite Ice's most eligible bachelor, Jackson Owen.

A star goalie with a lucky glove and a cocky smile, Jackson is exactly the kind of distraction I can't afford. But fate, with its twisted sense of humor, keeps throwing us together. The more I resist, the more I realize—maybe life has a different game plan for me.

And, well . . . the chemistry? It's undeniable.

Come and Get Your Glove is a will-they-or-won't-they, sweet hockey romcom that reminds readers love can find you in the most unexpected ways—even when you're doing everything in your power to fight it.

*As with all the books in this series, this is completely standalone.

One

Jackson Owen

"Bill Baker!" Noah yells before he bursts through the locker room doors. His mouth opens in a pant, and he scans the room. "Have you seen Bill?"

"Ah, no." I shake my head as I dig through my locker again, looking for my lucky glove. I never used to lose any of my stuff, but ever since my last breakup, my mind has been so distracted. I lost my glove last week before the game, and Bill grabbed a new one for me. It turned out that was a super lucky glove because we won that game. I definitely don't want to lose it. A knot swells in my throat when I lift my hockey bag again and look under it. Something drops to the floor. I don't even need to check to know it's my lucky glove. A sigh of relief falls from my lips.

I stuff my glove into my hockey bag and shift my gaze to Noah, who sniffs around the locker room like a bloodhound. "What's up, bruh?" I take a step back, hugging the lockers, as sometimes he gets like this when he's off his meds. "You okay?"

"No." His eyes are glossed over, and his face is crimson as he spins on his heel and shouts toward Bill's office. "Bill, you'd better get out here!"

I swallow, not understanding how he could talk to his boss like that and doubting that Bill is even here. Everybody left but me, and I'm only here because I've been scouring the place for my glove.

A shuffle from the door pulls both Noah's and my attention that way. It's Bill, dressed in head-to-toe Granite Ice warmup clothes. He leans against the wall and crosses his arms in front of him as if he's preparing for a confrontation.

"Tell me you didn't," Noah hisses, his expression so full of hatred that I do a double take. This is not the Noah I know. I'm about to push my hand on his chest to hold him back. He looks as if he's about to attack Bill.

"Noah," Bill says calmly. "I love you like a son, but I can't have you on my team while you're dating Blake's daughter."

My gaze bounces from Bill to Noah as I struggle to fill in the gaps. Noah blurts out everything I need to know. "You traded me." Noah's arms flail around as if he's having trouble controlling his body. "To some brand-new team nobody has even heard of."

"It's going to work out just fine." Bill's words are cool and measured. "You wanted to move out of the house and have your own life, didn't you? Well, this will get you all the way to Long Island. I traded you to Blake Anton's new team."

My jaw plummets all the way down.

Bill has lost his mind.

"Blake doesn't have a team." Noah rushes out, wild arm gestures continue to fly all around him. "And even if he did, why would you trade me?"

"Now you get to be with Paisley." Bill's smooth gesture seems almost condescending when paired with how upset Noah is. "Isn't that what you wanted?"

"N-no. It's not what I wanted. What I wanted was for you to accept Paisley as part of my life—the same way I accepted you as part of my mom's life." Noah stutters for a moment before spouting off, "This trade makes us rivals."

"No." Bill tips his head coyly at Noah. "You made us rivals when you started dating that woman."

Lightning could crash into this locker room, and it would be less shocking than what I'm seeing. I knew Noah had a new girlfriend, but I had no idea about the conflict going on behind the scenes. The tension in the air is palpable, and my gaze bounces from Noah to Bill.

"Whatever," Noah mutters as he slams his fist into a nearby locker. The echo fills the room. He doesn't wait for it to quiet before he storms out of the room, calling back, "You thought you were losers before, just wait until we meet again on the ice . . ."

Well, this is awkward. I tap my finger on my leg, pretending I didn't just witness the single most terrifying thing to go down since I joined this team. Bill is staring after the trail Noah left, and his cheeks are redder than a firetruck.

One thing I've learned about Bill is that you never want to cross him. I hug my hockey bag close to my chest, peeking inside to check for my glove. No relief comes over me this time, as the stakes have just been raised.

I might need two lucky gloves for next season . . .

Two

Jackson

I've trained my eyes not to blink. I can go for a full minute if I'm fueled on adrenaline like I am now. My eyes narrow on my opponent's winger as he skates in all cocky and fires a slap shot toward my net. The puck's trajectory is aimed precisely at the left center of the net—a shot I've blocked countless times. My mind tracks the split seconds it takes until it reaches me, drumming them like a bass in my ears. Holding my breath, I dive for the puck with my glove outstretched, ready for the win.

The deafening cheers of the crowd hollow and fade into background echoes as time stands still. My eyes are locked on the puck whizzing directly toward me in slow motion. With a healthy thud, it slams into my glove. My fingers tighten around it, and I let out a grunting sigh from the impact. While my teammates swarm around me, celebrating by pushing their gloves forward for knuckies, I thank my lucky glove. It's corny, I know, but there is something about this glove that prevents me from missing a catch.

It doesn't mean we win all the games. In fact, last season was quite the opposite as we lost most of our games.

But when it comes to catching pucks, I've never missed one with this glove.

Now, we're five goals ahead. With only seconds left on the clock, I can finally taste the win. It's our season opener, and I'm determined to have a better season than we had last season. Axl, our team center, pushes his knuckles toward me before whipping around and skating back to center ice for the final faceoff.

Elijah—the new winger—hangs back for a second, eyeing my glove. He's eighteen and fresh off his parents' farm. He's no Noah—the teammate he replaced—but he's catching on quickly. "I heard you said that glove was lucky, but now I believe it."

I nod, seeing clearly how this season is going to go.

We will destroy everyone.

"Mapleton has the lead," the announcer voice calls over the speakers, "Six to one." The crowd's cheering ticks even louder as the teams line up for one last faceoff. Axl quickly takes control of the puck and drives down the ice with speed. Then he drops it back to Elijah, who takes off in a breakaway and shoots the puck toward the net. Their goalie blocks it. Axl snags it on the rebound and shoots again. The puck flies past the diving goalie and into the net!

The buzzer blares, and the game is over. The benched players hop the wall, racing to center ice where we all gather in celebration.

Not only did we win, but it wasn't even close.

My chest puffs full of air that smells like sweat, but it's the best feeling in the world. My body aches from the strain of the game. With my leg muscles twitching, I skate toward the tunnel. My fingers curl in my glove, cupping nothing but air. It feels amazing.

Back in the locker room, Coach Carlson hugs the wall while the team owner, Bill Baker, puts a boot up on the bench in front of him. He leans forward while scanning the room. "Guys, we didn't just win a game. We finally proved to everyone—including ourselves—what we are capable of when we come together."

Some of the guys cheer, but I stay silent with my focus unwavering on Bill as he speaks over the cheers. "It couldn't have come at a better time, too. We can take this momentum into our next game. As you know, next we play Noah's new team, Arctic Force. We've put in the work. I guarantee you that they are putting in hard work too. All this week, I want to see you on the ice early. Leave your personal problems at home, focus on the ice, and trust your teammates so we can be ready to dominate them." Bill curls his fingers into a fist and shakes it in front of his chest. "No late nights. Nothing to distract you." He drops his foot off the bench and stands tall, scanning his gaze over us.

I nod when Bill makes eye contact.

I get it.

There was some drama that went down with Bill and Noah. Bill is not only Noah's stepdad, but he traded Noah to a rival team. All teams have rivalry, but let's just say Bill takes his competitive spirit to the next level. I've heard many stories about the things he's done. I've learned I don't want to upset him. That's why I stand back when Bill strides out the door, leaving us in silence. A few side conversations break out, but I move to the side bench and start to remove my gear.

Some days I feel like I play a completely different game than everyone else. They play a team sport. When I'm standing alone in front of a net, it's a solo sport with the whole game riding on my shoulders. In Bill's speech today, he said we won because "we came together" and the credit is shared. However, when we lose, the energy in this room is so thick and someone usually mumbles how the loss is my fault for letting the goals slip by.

It's not a team sport then.

I stuff my gear in my hockey bag, making sure to double check that my lucky glove is right on top. I let out a sigh of relief when I finally zip my bag, as if tonight's game is sealed. We start this season with a victory. I rise to my feet, shoulder my bag, and lumber out the door.

Axl raises his face as I pass by. "See ya."

I nod but don't speak as I exit the locker room. I've been told that goalies are a different breed. When I was younger it used to upset me because I wanted to feel like I belonged on the team. But, lately I'm starting to agree. There is something sadistic about willingly jumping in front of a soaring puck. Not to mention that I'm always a bit of a loner as a goalie. When everyone flies around the ice, working the puck together, I'm over in the net by myself. Sure, the defenders skate around, but nobody else is using their body to physically block the puck. I shrug to nobody, but it's a bit of needed stress relief. Maybe there is something a little off about me?

I reach Victory Hall, and my lips curl into a smile as I see my sister, Jackie, standing with my nephew, Rigsby. At only seven years old, he's a stud all decked out in Granite Ice hockey merch that is complemented with a fruit punch mustache over his upper lip. As soon as his eyes land on me, he dashes forward, soles of his sneakers squeaking as they slide on the tile dotted with small puddles from melted snow people tracked in. "Uncle Jack," he yells in an octave that's level with his game-cheering shout as he runs forward, not slowing his speed one bit. Instead of letting him crash into me, I drop my hockey bag, swipe him up mid-stride, and trap him against my hip.

"Whoa, buddy." I twist him around as I try to tickle his belly, but he squirms and covers his stomach with his arms and playfully kicks at me. "What do you think you're doing trying to attack me?" I tip him upside down and lower his face to the ground, teasing like I'm going to drop him. His laughter mixes with mine, and I swing him around and around until I'm dizzy. I flip him upright, lower his feet to graze the floor, and I let go.

He stands up, doing an exaggerated wobble. "Whoa, I'm dizzy now."

Jackie is finally within arm's reach, and she snatches Rigsby's hand to still him. With her free hand, she passes a small backpack to me. "Pajamas and clothes for tomorrow. His homework folder is also in there, and that needs to go with him to school tomorrow. It has his permission slip for his field trip, and we are already late turning it in."

"Got it." My hand drops from the surprising weight of the bag. I give it a double take as it feels as if it contains a bowling ball. "Send his pajamas to school tomorrow, and he needs a permission slip to sleep." Jackie's lips pinch into a strained smirk while her eyes nervously shift back to Rigsby. "Relax." I reach out, patting her shoulder. "He's going to be fine. I can handle a boy for the night."

"It's just that I've never left him before. Not for an overnight." She shifts her weight from leg to leg while she pats her pregnant belly, nine months huge.

"He's not a baby. He's seven, and you're getting induced in the morning. You deserve a night off from being parents before the new baby comes." I reach over and playfully squeeze the back of Rigsby's shoulder. A smile springs onto his face in reflex, and he roguishly taps a light kick to my shin. I hop back a full foot, preventing him from kicking me again, and flash a mischievous smirk at him. "You want to go, bud?"

"No killing each other in public," Jackie says in playful warning. Rigsby and I both pinch back smirks, pretending to get serious. Roughhousing is our favorite pastime. It's my mission to wear him out to the point of exhaustion until he begs to go to bed.

"Fine." I adjust his school bag while giving it another side-eye. I don't remember schoolbooks weighing this much. When I slug my hockey bag over the same shoulder, I feel like I'm getting a workout just standing here. I tap Rigsby on the shoulder and take a giant sidestep. "Should we grab root beers and wings at The Grove?"

That's all it took for Rigsby to close the gap as he steps away from his mom, calling back, "Bye, Mom."

"Don't I get a hug?" Her bottom lip drops in a pout, and she reaches forward. Rigsby leans on one leg to reach for her. For the briefest of moments, he squeezes her neck and then replants himself back by my side. "We're getting BBQ, right?"

"Any flavor you want." I slide a hand behind his back, guiding him forward, and call over my shoulder back to Jackie, "I got this."

Her feet stay cemented. I'm not dragging this out any longer. She'll come up with an excuse why she can't leave him, and she deserves this time with her husband. I continue to pace forward, hyping Rigsby up for the wings, "They have boneless and bone in, or you can try their new flavor—Cajun crusted—which will blow your mind and possibly your tongue off."

Rigsby is nothing but smiles. In my peripheral vision, I see Jackie finally starting to walk toward the main parking lot in the front of the building. I let out a sigh of relief. This is a big step for her, but she has nothing to worry about.

I'm great with kids.

Not even just a little great.

I'm like one of those Supernannies on TV.

We stride through the double sliding door together, and I brace myself for the gust of icy wind. The weather has gotten so much colder this last week. I glance down to check on Rigsby, his pudgy hand sliding in front of his stomach. It's an insignificant move that I assume helps to keep him warm, like giving yourself a big old bear hug. It's what he does next that makes me stop dead in my tracks. Bending at the waist, he juts his chin out like he's a duck who is about to quack. Only he's not a duck. I get a front row seat to the projectile vomit that spews from his mouth.

"Whoa." I slide behind him and grab his shoulders holding him steady. "You okay?" I resist looking down, focusing on him instead. Nope, the smell is enough. I do not need to get an up-close look at it.

"Better now." His hand clenches at his throat as if it's holding back an encore. "I got dizzy when you tipped me upside down."

My gaze travels over his winter coat, soiled all down the front. The good news appears that his coat absorbed everything. There is no mess anywhere else. He's definitely going to need a clean coat for school tomorrow. I don't have anything close to his size at my apartment, but there's a laundromat down the block from The

Grove. We could easily stop there and do a quick wash before we eat. "Well, if you are sure that you're feeling better, let's get in my car where it's warm." I wrap my arm around his shoulders to escort him. "We'll stop by the laundromat to wash your coat."

"What about the chicken wings?" It's a classic rebuttal I've learned to expect from Rigsby. I smirk at the top of his tousled hair.

"After we wash your coat." He drags his feet through fresh powder as if his legs don't bend at the knees. Somehow, we make it to my car without any more issues. He insists on taking his bag from me before he gets in the back seat. I drop my bag into the trunk. Getting my parenting groove back, I hop in the driver's seat and get a heavy whiff of puke and gag so hard I have to roll my window down. When that doesn't do the trick, I tug my shirt over my nose to muffle the stench. "What do you think after we eat, we stay up and watch wrestling?" I ask as I pull out of my spot and steer toward the street.

"Mom says I have to go to bed by eight." His tone is matter of fact; his jaw locked.

"Right." A mischievous smile buds on my lips. Jackie can't expect me to be the funcle by following all her boring rules. "I won't tell your mom."

His eyes swell round and huge, finding mine in the rearview mirror, and he doesn't mouse a word. I turn the classic rock radio station louder than normal. With the arena being out of town, it's a short drive back to Mapleton. We rock all the way back until I swerve into a parking spot about a block from the laundromat. Popping my door open, I drop a foot to the street and call back, "Alright, bud, let's get this coat taken care of."

I hadn't thought about it before, but I realize my hockey gear has to be equally stinky, and I grab it to make efficient use of my time. We walk to the door, and I open it, stepping back to allow him to pass first.

As I scan the small room, I'm overwhelmed. It's wall to wall people, and every machine seems to be taken. "Who would have thought it would be so busy?" I point my gaze at Rigsby, but the question is aimed more at myself. My hungry stomach churns. It's not happy about this delay, but I don't have a choice but to wait for a machine. I can't make my nephew walk around with a puke-covered coat at school. I also won't call his mom for a backup, because she's hopefully enjoying her evening off.

I spike my hand through my hair, scanning the room one more time for a place for us to wait. An elderly lady in the far corner has removed the last of her clothes from her machine and shuts the door. I grab Rigsby's hand and propel him forward. "Let's get this machine." We weave through the narrow row until we reach it. I drop my hockey bag on the bench across from the machine and unzip it, pulling out my jersey and pants.

Rigsby plops down on the bench as I shuffle items into the machine. When it's full, I pat my jacket pocket, and...no familiar lump of my wallet. I turn back to the door. "I must have left my wallet in the car," I mumble. My gaze wafts back to the gear. I hate to leave it out like this. Mapleton's a safe little town, but I'm not risking my gear getting stolen.

With an impatient sigh, I remove my items from the machine, stuff them back into my bag, and scan the aisle again for something to save my machine so nobody takes it.

Just my luck.

There's a single cart left. I retrieve it and park it next to my machine. I also leave the door wide open. I'm a little genius like that because now it looks occupied. "Alright, bud." I place a hand on his shoulder. "I know it's gross but leave your coat on for another minute. We have to run back to my car to grab my wallet."

He gives me one of those looks that says, "I'm getting hungrier by the second," and I add, "We're doing a quick-wash cycle, and we'll be out of here in an hour." When he doesn't reply, I tack on, "And you can have unlimited root beer." Finally, he scrambles to his feet, eagerly plodding toward the door.

"Let's hurry." I scurry as I swipe my hand over my forehead, wiping the sheen of sweat. I've only had this kid in my care for twenty minutes, and I'm already feeling stressed.

Three

KACI ROBERTS

I tap the brake of my Honda CRV to coast over the smooth asphalt of the Mapleton police parking lot. It's past sunset, the time of night where only a soft glow of auburn shadows the underbelly of the dark sky. My eyes are peeled as I scan from left to right, hoping once in my unlucky life that Chase could be on time.

It's Sunday night. I just clocked out of a twelve-hour shift, waitressing at The Grove restaurant. I'm excited to spend some time with Bella tonight before school starts tomorrow, but if Chase doesn't get here soon, he's going to cut into my time.

I loathe—with a capital L—these transfers.

I loathe the sight of Chase.

I loathe the sound of his gritty voice.

I loathe that he pulls up in his jacked-up truck, which is completely impractical for having a seven-year-old in tow. I can't begin to think how much money he's dumped into that road hazard, all the while complaining about how he can't make child support.

I loathe that he blares awful death metal music, and I cringe when he doesn't turn it down when Bella gets in the truck.

Let's not forget that drama is Chase's shadow's personal name. He's always got a story about why he is never where he agreed to be, and of course it's never his fault.

Even if all of that was miraculously fixed today, he's unrelenting at sucking the life out of my soul.

And just as I thought.

Tonight is not any different.

He's not where he agreed to be.

With no sign of him anywhere, I let out a hefty huff and pull into the spot closest to the front door—right next to a police cruiser. Since he plays this game to get under my skin, I resist the urge to text to find out where he is.

Instead, I reach across the passenger seat to rifle through my backpack until I find my music theory textbook. I'm not a nerd who geeks out on this stuff. However, I am in the final semester of my bachelor's degree in music education, and I have my first exam tomorrow. It's always been my dream to teach. Sure, it's an ordinary job that doesn't seem like a huge stretch or even that big of a goal, but I've completed all my classes while single parenting and working. It's been a long haul to get here—taking me twice as long as traditional students. It's been almost a full eight years, and not one of them was easy, but I never gave up. Now, I have two more classes to pass, and I'll finally have a professional job with normal hours and health insurance. I'm hoping desperately that it leads to a more stable life for Bella and me.

Because it has to.

I've put all my hope into this degree.

I'm careful not to look in the mirror when I tap the overhead light on. Car mirrors hurt my feelings. I slouch in my seat to get comfortable and flip through my book until I find the chapter on assessments. I drop my index finger to the page and force my tired eyes to follow along as I read, "Educational assessment is a systematic process of documenting and using evidence to improve educational programs and studen—" My chin slams to my chest, jolting me awake. I didn't even make it a full sentence, and I'm already nodding off.

I need some air.

I press the window control, lowering it enough to allow in a breath of fresh air. Loud back beats thrum behind me. There's no need to turn around to know Chase has finally returned with my child. Popping the door open, I slide out and stand next to the empty spot that he pulls into. He strides around from his side of the truck with a garbage bag in his hand. "Here you go." He drops the bag to the asphalt without breaking eye contact with me. The corners of his mouth twitch like he's doing everything he can not to smirk.

"What is that?" As if I'm afraid to look at it, I also don't let my gaze stray away from his face. A smug sneer fills in the bottom half of his face, and he looks like an absolute tool. I cringe. *I can't believe I used to love this guy.*

"It's Bella's dirty laundry. I didn't have time to wash it."

"Thank you." My voice laces with sarcasm as I resist reminding him that doing Bella's laundry from his days is in our custody agreement. I've learned he doesn't care. With Bella in the truck, I refuse to waste my precious time with her on his deficiencies. He's the one with an in-home washer and dryer, and doing laundry for him is pretty painless. I, on the other hand, must use the laundromat—which I'm grateful to have right down the street from my apartment—but it's not my job to do his chores.

But I don't tell him that.

Instead, I take the garbage sack and walk it to the back of my car, pop the hatch, and toss it in.

"What's wrong, Kaci?" His words slur together, like he's about to mock me.

"What makes you think something's wrong?" I slam the trunk shut and walk around to his truck, open the back door, step up on the guard rail, and bite my bottom lip—hard.

Bella's head droops forward, and her eyes are sealed. It's way too late for a nap, not to mention she gave up napping years ago. Chase knows this ruins my plans for an early bedtime, but again I don't let him see my frustration. I tap her shoulder, and call softly, "Bella, baby, it's time to get up."

Her dark lashes flutter open, allowing the brightest shade of blue to peek out. A sleepy smile pins on her lips. "Mom," she calls as she throws her slender arms around my neck, pulling me close. Her hug makes this painful exchange with Chase worth it.

"Baby, it's time to come with me."

She's my perfect angel. Obedient to me in a way I don't deserve as she happily unlatches her seatbelt, grabs her stuffed bear, Little B, and climbs out of the truck, latching her fingers in between mine. It's a tight squeeze with the two vehicles parked so close together. My shoulder brushes against Chase's as I pass in front of him. Of course he's got something to say. "Girl, you smell like stress and dirty dishes."

Normally I can let anything he says roll right off me, but I tilt my head and replay what he said.

I've been called a hot mess before, but wow, this is something else.

The sad thing is that it doesn't sting. He's probably right. I just got off work. Not to mention, it's been ages since I allowed myself the funds to purchase any personal care products other than soap, shampoo, and the very basics of drugstore makeup. I definitely don't wear perfume or even scented lotion; they're not in my budget. I steel my expression, locking away all my emotions from bearing. I've long since been a closed book for him. I don't care to exchange any personal talk. "Next Friday, Bella has her school fall harvest festival," I inform him, as I highly doubt he opens the emails from Bella's teacher. "Would you like to do transition at the school after that?"

He shuts the backdoor of his truck and casually leans his shoulder to rest against it. "Why not?" He offers me a smile one could argue is diplomatic, but I know him all too well.

"Okay, Friday at the school," I repeat as I slide into my driver's seat and close the door, shutting out him and any chance of a rebuttal. I snap my seatbelt on, check my rearview mirror, and my heart instantly refuels when my gaze plants on Bella beaming back at me. "How was your dad's house?"

Her perfect button nose scrunches, leaving little lines to dot between her eyes. It's an animation she's made since she was a baby, and it reminds me of my mom. Genetics is a funny thing. I used to wonder why she didn't inherit any of my mannerisms, but now I don't question it. All she needs is a perfect set of acrylic nails and a blow-dried, fluffy hairdo, and she'd be a perfect twin to my mom.

It's not a bad thing.

My mother might have more sense than me. She warned me about Chase in the beginning, again in the middle, and even the end. Clearly, I didn't listen. I shift the car into reverse, ignore the weird ticking sound that seems to be coming from the floorboards and slowly back out. Since she still hasn't replied to my question, I rephrase it: "Did you do anything fun?"

"We went to band practice." She positions Little B in the center of her lap and proceeds to straighten the tattered red ribbon around the bear's neck. That bear was the first stuffed animal I gave her when she was only a few days old. I've offered to replace it, and have certainly bought her many other stuffed animals over the years, but nothing takes the place of Little B.

"Band practice?" I flick my blinker on and turn left. Chase has dabbled with all sorts of musical instruments as he has a talent to play by ear. Music was the one thing that brought us together, and we always had that in common. He really is a talented musician. I'll give him that much, but he has a terrible time sticking to anything. Every band he's ever been a part of has kicked him out after he missed too many practices. "Which band?"

Her shoulders rise and fall, and her focus never leaves Little B. "It was in some dude's basement."

Nice.

I bite back my sarcasm. More than likely the band was not appropriate for a seven-year-old to hear. We've reached Main Street, and I pull to the side of the road right in front of the laundromat. "Alright, dear." I sigh as I unclick my seatbelt and reach for my purse. "This was not my plan, but you need clean clothes for school. Let's get everything washed up. Since it's already almost bedtime, we can order dinner while we are here."

Her gaze shifts to the neon lights above the brick building spelling "Laundromat." The neon M appears to be shorting out—blinking on for a few seconds before it darkens for an even longer pulse, then repeating the pattern. It's the only way I've ever remembered the building to look. "I hate going here." Her tone isn't ungrateful. It's akin to inflections you'd hear from someone who blew all their birthday candles but one. Not disappointment at all, but more of an observation.

I don't tell her that we wouldn't have to waste time here if her dad had done his own chores. Nope, I don't say that at all. I aim a smile at her. "What kind of pizza would you like?"

An immediate sparkle returns to the center of her eyes, reflecting hues of blue so vibrant they look made up. "Extra cheese?"

"Anything you want." I walk to the back of the car, retrieve the garbage bag, and step on the curb to wait for her to walk with me toward the blinking M.

We pass through the front door and are hit by a cacophony of machines running all along the walls. My senses are immediately overloaded by the small crowd of people. There seems to be a person sitting in front of every machine. It's a small laundromat, but I've never had problems finding an open machine before. Who knew Sunday night at the laundromat would be so popular?

I grab Bella's hand, and we shimmy sideways to fit through the narrow aisle between the benches of people and the machines. Most of the people are about college age, which now makes sense to me as to why they opted for Sunday night to do laundry. I know

I've never seen any of these people here on Saturday mornings, when I usually do my laundry.

Scanning the back wall for an open machine, I'm about to lose hope when I see one machine in the far corner with the front door open. I rise to the tips of my toes to check inside, and my heart pumps with excitement.

It's empty.

I tug on Bella's hand, pulling her a little faster in hopes of getting to it before someone else. "We are in luck," I exclaim as we close the gap between us and the machine. A forgotten cart is pushed up against it. I look all around to see who it belongs to, but there isn't anyone here who appears to care about it.

Bella drops onto the narrow bench in front of the machine, and I plop my bag into the cart and sort through the laundry, removing the colored clothes first and adding them to the machine. Half the clothes in the bag do not even look as if they'd fit Bella anymore. The more I rummage, the more I realize that Chase added everything to this bag. There's no way she wore all this stuff in the three days she had him.

He's like a child who always goes out of his way to annoy me.

It's not going to work.

I take a deep breath and calmly add the rest of the clothes to the machine, swipe my card to pay, and stand back as the clothes start to tumble around. Everything looks good, so I turn back to Bella. "Alright, I bet you're hungry. Let's order food." Her expression remains unchanged, and my heart pings, deflating a little. This wasn't the fun mother-daughter night I had planned for us. Bella's slumped shoulders tell the truth that she's feeling the same way.

Forcing a cheery voice, I raise my eyebrows and tack on, "Maybe we can watch a movie on my phone?"

Her posture perks up a little, but her eyes are glazed over the way they get when she's tired. I'm sure she didn't get the rest she needed since Chase doesn't care about bedtimes. I hate this so much, but I refuse to let it ruin our night. I retrieve my phone from my purse, tap on the pizza app, cruise through my clicks to order a pizza, and then hand my phone to her. "Go ahead and pick out a movie. The pizza should be here in twenty minutes."

Her fingers brush against mine as I slide my phone to her. Finally the tips of her lips bend up in a genuine smile—a tired smile, but a smile nonetheless. Since I'm not in a winning-at-life era, I always count the small wins.

That is one for the day.

"Wait a second . . ." A baritone voice calls as measured footsteps stop right behind me. "Who took my machine?" I toss a lazy look over my shoulder and do a double take as I observe a *hot guy*.

He's got an athletic build, muscular ripples in all the right places, and he's standing next to a small boy who looks to be about Bella's age. The boy is adorable as any kid that age is, but the dude is so freakishly handsome it causes me to freeze.

With his chiseled jawline and full lips, he could seriously be a model.

His eyes are a rare shade of blue-green, and his hair is medium brown with light blond tips as if he spends days at the beach. He and the boy are dressed in dark blue sweatpants and jackets like they are part of some sports team. When I narrow my gaze, I see a Granite Ice logo on the guy's coat.

The ripples make sense now.

After a beat of silence, where I pretend to not be looking at how wide his shoulders are, he repeats his question, "Who took my machine?"

My lips pinch tight, puckering in the middle. It's beyond rude to take someone's machine. Everyone is busy. I can't stand people who try to cheat to get ahead, but it's not my business to interfere. I turn my gaze down, pinning it onto my phone to help Bella scroll for a movie to watch.

His feet shuffle forward, stopping only when his hand lands on *my machine,* and his gaze slams onto me. "Did you take my machine?"

"I beg your finest pardon." Defensiveness buds in my chest, and I straighten my spine to sit taller. I'm not exactly petite at five foot five, but I've learned to exaggerate my height when I'm trying hard to get a point across. "That's my machine."

"Well, no. It's mine. I reserved it." His tone is extra curt as he slices his hand through the air in my direction. "I parked my cart in front of it to hold it while I went back to my car for my wallet." His gaze scans the immediate surroundings until it lands on *my cart* still half-filled with laundry and my garbage bag. He effortlessly steps forward and taps his palm on the cart, saying in a commanding voice, "This is my cart. You took that too." His eyes scan top to bottom before a disgusted sigh escapes out of his lips, and he grumbles, "Apparently, you put garbage in it."

I suck in a giant inhalation, holding all my overwhelming emotions.

This guy is delusional.

The cart didn't have *his* name on it. It didn't have anything to mark that it belonged to anybody. It was empty.

Like the washing machine, it was empty.

I run my palm over my hair, smoothing it down, hoping to calm the quibbles sparking in my gut. Can he not see how arrogant he's being? You can't walk into a business and claim something when it doesn't have your money, your laundry or your name on it. He has about as much right to this washing machine as I have right to the Empire State Building. None. "There wasn't any money or anything in it," I spout back and shrug an exhausted shoulder.

Did I really care that much about a washing machine?

No.

On any other day, I'd walk away. Tonight is my one night to hang out with Bella. I'm wasting our time here because of stupid Chase. It's not fair, and I want this chore done. Now. "Guess you'll have to wait for the next one."

His gaze drifts to the boy next to him, and they both execute a childish eye roll. Apparently, they are on the same mental maturity level. I turn my head away, refusing to give him a second glance.

Okay, maybe a little glance when he pivots. I have to double check how his jaw looked from this angle.

Seriously, nobody's jaw is that perfect.

He must be pushing his chin out just to be annoying.

I overhear him tell the boy that they'll leave to eat. I let out a quiet breath and return my attention to Bella, who's staring at me intently. "What?" I ask, blinking several times to declare my innocence. "I didn't take his machine. You saw it was empty."

"That's Rigsby Kane. A kid in my class." She jerks her head toward the door, sending her ponytail flipping in that direction.

"Oh," is all I manage. I vaguely remember the kid now that she's mentioned it. I've seen his mom drop him off at school. I'm just so tired and disappointed about how this night is going. Even my lashes feel heavier than normal as I lock my gaze on Bella, leaning over my phone as she zones out on the movie she selected.

Maybe I was a little rude?

It wasn't my fault.

Maybe he thought he had saved the machine, but again, he didn't do it well enough. It wasn't obvious.

Plus, I'll never see them again.

Exhausted, I am mentally disengaged as Bella watches the movie. It's almost over when her clothes are done drying. I rush to fold them and carefully put them back in the garbage bag, since I don't have any other way to carry them. I'm slowly getting my sense of humor back. I know this because I let out a disgusted chuckle when I tie up the bag. It's almost nine, and I'm completely bummed that we didn't have any time to relax together at home. Trying to hide my disappointment, I once again force a smile. "Alright, clothes are clean. We can go."

She stands up, but her gaze drops to the floor. She immediately bends over and reaches between the washing machines and pulls out something. "Look, it has the same logo that guy's jacket had." Pushing it forward, she lines the logo up with my gaze. "I bet it is his."

"Maybe?" Tilting my head, I examine it. It's a giant glove. She's right. It's an identical match to his jacket.

"We need to let him know we have it." Her tone toggles between telling and asking. I should be proud she's growing into such a responsible young lady, but it pings at my heart that she puts such worries on herself.

She inherited that from me.

Worrying. It's my superpower.

I worry so much, I worry about my worrying.

"Uh, I don't know about that." I lift the bag out of the cart and slug it over my shoulder. My head is pounding from the longest day ever, and the last thing I want to do is run after someone who was careless enough to lose his stuff.

This glove, I will not worry about.

This is the one time I draw the line on my worrying.

I jerk my thumb over my shoulder, motioning to the machines. "We can leave it on top of the machine. He'll come back for it if he needs it."

"Mom, if we leave it here, someone might take it." Her tone is extra curt, mirroring the one I give her when she isn't listening. "Rigsby goes to my school. I can literally take it to him."

"Fine," I murmur, taking the glove from her with a straight elbow as if I'm afraid to touch it. That guy was annoying. He doesn't deserve a favor, but I am a role model. And maybe I did use the machine he *thought* he saved.

"You should message Rigsby's mom on Facebook so she knows." She hands my phone to me, screen side up.

My brows bead together as I now worry about her worrying too much. She's right though. It's a small town, and I've seen that mom in the drop-off lane at school many times. I know what she looks like. I think her first name is Jackie. "I mean, I guess I can." I take my phone and open Facebook. "Did you say his last name is Kane?"

"Yeah."

I quickly search for people with that name in Mapleton, and just my luck—I find a woman whose profile picture shows a kid who looks like Rigsby. I impatiently type.

Me: Hey, Jackie. You don't know me, but our kids go to school together. I saw Rigsby at the laundromat tonight, and the man he was with left a hockey glove. Not sure if it's important, but I have it if he needs it.

"Let's go home." I'm about to slip my phone into my coat pocket when a vibration stops me.

Jackie: Yes, that would be my brother, Jackson. He's watching Rigsby for the night. I'll let him know you have it.

Me: I'll bring it to school tomorrow.

I pause, making sure our conversation is over. When I get no more notifications, I set my gaze back on Bella. "Alright, sweetie, we can finally go home."

Four

JACKSON

Shaking my head, I look down at my phone. Apparently, I didn't hear my alarm go off, because it's twenty minutes past the time I set it for. This is not a good way to start the day. I drop my feet to the ground, grab a Granite Ice hoodie from my closet, and throw it over my head. Of all the days to oversleep, why must it be when I have Rigsby? I hurry from my room and go straight to the couch.

"Rigsby," I say softly. He doesn't even twitch, so I repeat it a bit louder: "Rigsby, get up." He's flat on his back, one hand above his head, his slobbery bottom lip hanging open like he's sacked out after a long night of partying. To be fair, I didn't get him to bed at the time I was told to. I ignored Jackie's warnings about how tough mornings are when he doesn't sleep. I didn't think his ears wouldn't work.

With my phone in one hand, I reread the text I got last night.

Jackie: Apparently some girl from Rigsby's class found your hockey glove at the laundromat. She said she'll bring

it to school in the morning if you want to look for her. She messaged me on Facebook about it. The mom's name is Kaci.

My throat had cinched tight.

That's my lucky glove!

I didn't know I had lost it. After reading the text, I ran to my bag and dumped it out. The glove wasn't there, and my heart slammed against my chest—where it's stayed ever since. If I hadn't already been warned that it was gone, I might have had a heart attack. I'm so lucky to know where it is.

If I had my way, I would have gone last night when I got the text, but it was late, and Jackie never gave me a number to reach out to the girl or her parents. I also didn't want to bother Jackie on her last night before the baby arrives.

Besides, I know who has the glove. It's the girl with the woman who stole my machine.

I cringe when I think about that interaction. I was confused about my machine, and acting out of character, but something happened when I focused on that woman. She was a sonic boom to my brain, an unexpected beauty, with fair skin and trim body, except for her hips, which were full in my favorite way. I don't normally go looking for women, as I'm enjoying my bachelor era. She was definitely a reminder that just because I'm enjoying being single doesn't mean I can't admire beauty.

Until she opened her mouth.

No, there was nothing wrong with her voice, but the only sparks that flew were the ones that were hot off her attitude. Shaking my head, I mumble, "Yep, I'm fine admiring from a distance and not engaging."

My gaze flicks to the clock on my phone. I have no idea what time she will drop off her kid. I don't want to risk missing them. We need to leave early. According to Bill, tomorrow is the biggest game of the season. We can't lose to Arctic Force. *I need that glove.*

I urgently tap Rigsby's shoulder. "Hey, you've got to get up for school." His hand slides down until it covers his ear, more than likely to tune me out, and he rolls over to his side facing away from me.

This isn't working. I roll back my tight shoulders as I can't stop thinking about my glove. I can't be late and miss it. Tension pools in the front of my head.

Jackie was right about bedtime.

I stuff my phone in the middle pocket of my hoodie and lean over Rigsby. This time I'm not wasting time by tapping. I slide my arms around his waist and scoop him up like he's a giant sack of potatoes, slugging him over my shoulder as I walk toward the bathroom.

On cue, he mumbles, "Is it morning already?"

"Yeah, bud." I take a left into the small bathroom and set him in front of the sink. "Wash your face and get dressed. We'll grab some bagels and coffee on the way to school."

His brows bunch together, but his eyelids spring more open. "I don't drink coffee."

"Oh, yeah." I spread a playful smile on my lips. "You should because it would give you a reason to get out of bed in the morning." Pivoting, I turn toward the shower where I have his coat hung on the rail. We never made it back to the laundromat because it got too late. I was stuck washing his coat by hand in the sink. Just the thought of scrubbing out the vomit forces me to resist dry heaving.

Taking care of kids is quite disgusting.

I pull his coat down, checking it over for damp spots. It seems to be dry. It even has a nice fresh ivory smell from the dish soap I used since I was out of laundry soap. I usually buy the overpriced stuff at the laundromat, and it was too late to go back out. Apparently, I'm missing some sort of childcare checklist because I didn't know I should restock my laundry soap before Rigsby came.

His coat is extra-fragrant though.

"Alright, bud." I turn on my heel and head out to give him space. "Remember I need to get my glove. I haven't the slightest clue what time she'll be there. So, let's hurry." I toss a quick glance over my shoulder to make sure he's in motion. Instead of reaching to turn the faucet on, his hand finds his stomach. His already chubby cheeks puff full of air as his eyes waiver into a bit of a cross-eyed stare. "Rigsby," I say cautiously, "are you feeling okay?"

"Aw, I'm not sure." He's still as can be, looking as if he's afraid of what's about to happen.

"Do you need something to eat to settle your stomach? Maybe some juice?" I mentally take inventory of my fridge. Unfortunately, it's not the most kid friendly. I've got energy drinks, sushi, and leftover Chinese takeout.

"Nah, I don't want anything." His face blanches to ashen. I fumble for my phone to text Jackie, but then pause as I remember I told her I wasn't going to bother her. She's more than likely getting induced at this very moment. She doesn't need this situation on her plate too.

She never left me an instruction manual for this!

"What does your mom usually do when you feel like this? Do you go to a doctor or lie down?" I speak as my thumb hovers over my phone.

"She says I have a nervous stomach. Usually, she rubs my back and sings to me until I feel better."

"Well, I'm not going to sing to you, and trust me, you wouldn't want me to." I glance at my medicine cabinet, but I don't pause for long. There's nothing in it but cold medicine. I have a stomach of steel and have never had this issue. "Uh, new plan. Let's run to the drug store to get some Pepto-Bismol, before we meet that lady."

"What lady?" His brows furrow, and his lack of urgency is grating on my nerves.

"I don't remember her name," I speak quickly. "It's the gorgeous-but-oh-so-annoying lady from the laundromat who stole our machine."

I reach my hand out to him, coaxing him forward. "Can you come with me if we walk slowly? I'll bring a barf bag." It's not an ideal situation, but I must make it to that school. If he's still ill when I get my glove, I'll bring him back home, but at least I'll have my glove.

Five

KACI

The sun peeks through the clouds, bringing a ray of optimism that I haven't felt in days. Bella and I round the corner of our apartment building, en route to my assigned parking spot. My dream is to move to an apartment with a garage. More than likely a move won't be possible until I finish school.

Bella skips beside me wearing her favorite jean skirt and her Hello Kitty backpack slug over her shoulders. She insisted she needed to wear a skirt today, even though it's only thirty-five degrees. We settled on a compromise, and she put leggings underneath. She looks adorable with her braided pigtails and cheery smile, and, as always, she's carrying Little B.

I've loaded up my giant mom purse with the book I need for class, a water bottle, snacks, and the hockey glove. I'm not sure when I should give up on fitting everything into a purse and swap it out for a duffel bag. At least for today, I'm making the purse work.

I'm almost able to match Bella's smile until I spot my car, and my heart sinks.

"Mom, look!" Bella's index finger darts out, highlighting the very thing I'm staring at.

My back tire is flat.

It sometimes loses air from the cold, but this isn't a low tire situation. This is my rim resting against the cement, and I'm not going anywhere with my tire like this. I don't trust myself to put the spare on, so I'll have to call a service guy to take care of it. Normally that wouldn't be a big deal, but of course, this is the one day I can't be late dropping off Bella. We need to be early to meet the bus for her field trip.

As if reading my mind, Bella voices her worry. "What about my field trip?"

"Uh, we'll get there." I scan the parking lot for any neighbors who might be out and able to give us a ride to the school. It's not that far, but it's not something I'd attempt to walk in this weather.

My heart sinks another level.

Nobody is around.

"You know," I pull out my phone, "I'll request an Uber. That's what those things are for. Then while we get a ride to school, I'll have someone change my tire." I force an I'm-not-phased smile as a visible shiver runs through Bella's arms, and I nod toward the building. "Let's wait in the lobby."

We scramble back inside, bustling through the door at the same time. Anxiety courses through me. With my forehead pressed against the glass, I leave one hand on the door handle, watching for our ride.

This is not how I wanted this day to go.

"Why don't you call Dad to give us a ride?" Her question hits me like a cold bucket of ice water dumped over my head. Even my eyelids refuse to blink as if I'm frozen. I never know what to say in these situations. I'm trying hard not to discourage their relationship, but if there was ever a person who proved he wouldn't be there for me in this life—it was Chase.

"I'm sure he's at work already." I grit my teeth as I really have no idea if he even shows up to his job site. It seems to me that being a drywaller would be a flexible gig, but the last thing I ever want is to owe him any favors. He's the kind of guy who only helps when there is something to "transaction" with, and it always has to be in his favor. Her lashes lower to her cheeks the way they do when she's in trouble. "Bella, if you're worried about the field trip, don't be. We'll get there."

She pulls Little B closer to the center of her chest, hugging her tightly. "Nah, I was actually thinking about Dad."

"Oh." I don't want to ruminate on all the ways I had a baby with the wrong guy.

I know I made a mistake.

I'm not calling him to help me.

Not today.

Not any day.

But again, I try hard to support her relationship with him. "What about him?"

Her lashes rise, fluttering unsteadily as if she's doing everything to hold back her emotions. I slide my hand around her shoulder and pull her close. "Baby, what's on your mind? Did something happen when you were at Dad's house?"

"It's just . . . Don't take this the wrong way, Mom, but..." the pause she inserts in the middle of her sentence pings at my heart. Somewhere in the last year when she turned seven, she warped into this weird age where she's still seven, but going on thirty-five. "Sometimes I need a hug from Dad. You know, when I can't see him."

I fight hard to keep my brows steady and not frown. "That's okay if you feel that way. He's your dad." My words are soft as if they are meant to float in the air all day. I'm about to add how proud I am of her, but she breaks the silence.

"But I don't think he ever needs a hug from me." Her eyes, clear as crystals, latch onto mine, as if waiting for some words of wisdom.

My heart putters hard against my rib cage, and I run my tongue over my lips as I grapple to find the right words to say.

I know *exactly* how she feels.

It's the same way I felt when we were in a relationship. I never in a million years wanted my daughter to feel that way too.

She isn't talking *only* about hugs, either.

It's so much more than that.

It's how Chase only ever thinks of himself. "Well," my voice cracks, but I push through. "You know how he is. He's not much of—" I drop my sentence as the sound of car tires driving over compact snow pulls my attention. "That must be our ride," I mumble, straightening my overstuffed mom bag over my shoulder.

Bella steps forward, places one hand on the door handle, and we push it open. I'm not done with our conversation. I hate that my words don't come as fast as I want them to. I drop my hand to her shoulder. "Honey, you know I always have a hug for you, don't you?"

Her head turns up, and she latches her eyes on mine as we stride toward the car. "Sure, Mom. I know." She reaches the car first, opens the back door, and slides in. She scoots all the way over, removes her backpack, and sets it in the middle seat. When I slide in, I plop my purse next to the backpack and shut my door as quickly as possible.

"Good morning," I greet the driver, an elderly man who looks like he's almost too old to drive. "We need a ride to Mapleton Elementary today." I'm about to add a second stop at the college but decide I can easily walk to the campus from her school. It's only a few blocks, and I can save a couple of bucks.

"Is that the school downtown by the bookstore?" His voice is soothing, and I relax in my seat. My heart rate finally begins to slow. It's been a grueling morning, and it's not even eight yet.

"Nah." I shake my head, picturing downtown. "That's the private school. We need to go to the public school. It's on Applecart Avenue."

"Applecart," he echoes, still not pulling forward. My gaze drops to check the time on the phone clenched in my hand. Not late yet. We'll be cutting it close. It's not hard to navigate Mapleton. It's a small town with fewer than ten main roads. We need to leave now.

"Uh, yeah Applecart connects to Austin Street." I pause, feeling my heart pound faster. "Are you new to town?"

"Not really new, but I don't leave my apartment very much."

"That explains it." I lean forward and point through the opening between the front seats. "You can drive forward and turn left when you get to Green Avenue. That will take you to Austin. Then you take that to Applecart."

"Does that go by the train station?" His lips purse out as he waits for my response.

"Uh, no, not at all," I blurt out. "That's in the other direction. Why don't you start driving, and I'll let you know when to turn." When he still doesn't move, I add, "Please."

He finally shifts the car into drive and pulls forward at the slowest possible speed. I narrate the entire drive to make sure he doesn't take a wrong turn. When we reach the block before the school, I arch my chin and project my voice even louder, "Can you pull into the bus loop. We're supposed to meet up with the class there."

"Do you mean that bus?" His knobby finger trembles as he points over the steering wheel at a yellow school bus number nine crossing in front of the intersection where we are stopped.

My brows spring up, and my gaze slams toward Bella before trailing back to the taillights headed out toward the main highway. "Is that your bus?"

"Number nine!" Her voice rises in pitch, and her cheeks flush pink. "That's my class!"

"We can catch it!" I grab her hand, yanking her toward my door as I crack it open and drag her behind me. She clutches Little B to her chest as if it's her job to protect her. I wave my free arm wildly above my head and wail at the top of my lungs, "Come back!"

"It's no use, Mom," Bella's voice cracks under the weight of the tears she's holding back, and it fuels my legs to run toward the bus. There's a Stop sign up ahead. I'm not giving up. We will run as fast as we can and catch them while they're stopped.

"Let's run!" I continue to wave my hands and scream toward the bus. Bella and I race through the slushy snow-filled streets after the yellow streak ahead of us.

It's not that far.

If only the bus driver would look behind her, she'd see us. "Wait!" I scream again, my voice growing horse between the shrill volume and the icy air cutting at my throat. The bus makes a left turn onto the highway ramp and speeds up, disappearing. I slowly stop with one last splash in a slush puddle.

I stand still, staring forward because I can't look at Bella.

She had been talking about this field trip for weeks.

How could I let her down like this?

"It's okay, Mom." She tugs at my hand, pulling me back before I even look at her. "We tried."

It's times like these that I wish I was more irresponsible. I'd get in that Uber and follow that bus, but they are going all the way to Burlington, and the expense would kill me. Not to mention, I'd miss my exam.

My exam!

I run my shaking hand through my hair and pivot on my heel. "I can't be late for my class." My mind races a million miles an hour. I have no idea what to do with Bella while I'm in class. I don't exactly have a daycare I can take her to. I guess I'll just have to take her to class. We wasted so much time, I'll have the Uber take us back. My brows bend down as my eyes narrow, scanning the street, and my heart slams against my chest.

No Uber.

"Mom, what's wrong?" Bella's confusion doesn't slow her as we retrace our steps back to the school.

"That Uber left with our bags in it!" Her second-grade home-work isn't a big deal, but my super expensive college textbook is extremely important. Not to mention my wallet with my ID, my debit card, and my keys! Stupid Uber app! It takes payment directly from my app, and he never had to wait for me. He just left.

Oh, man.

This is getting worse by the minute. I swipe my hand through my hair again. This time, I resist the urge to yank on it and scream as we run all the way back to the bus loop, only to find it *empty*.

My eyes blur with tears. This has got to be the worst day ever. I turn in a circle frantically searching for a sign of which direction the Uber went.

The loop is empty.

Well, empty except for one car.

One shiny black car with nice silver rims, that just so happens to have a man and small child standing in front of it. A man wearing a Granite Ice jacket.

He waves at me as soon as he recognizes me, and a memory slams to the front of my brain—I'm supposed to give him his glove.

His glove is in my bag.

The bag that is in the Uber.

Uh, I hate this day so much.

I slowly face him, my chest tightening with dread.

"Did you miss the bus too?" he calls from his spot on the other side of the loop. Maybe it's the natural lighting, but he looks different this morning. He's still handsome, but his face is a tad scruffier than I remember. I squint but can't detect the color of his eyes. They definitely look bright today. Not as grumpy as last night. I pray he's not in a terrible mood because if he gives me grief about losing his glove, I won't be able to hold back. I did everything I could.

"I had a flat tire," I respond as we pace toward him, lowering my volume when we finally step on to the curb next to him. "I had to get an Uber. We got the *one driver* who either had dementia and forgot the streets of Mapleton, or it was his first day on the job."

"It sounds a lot like our morning." A hearty chuckle leaks out. I can't help but picture how that smile is going to deflate when he hears I lost his glove. Shaking his head, he replies, "Rigsby got a nervous stomach, and we had to stop at the drug store. There was only one checkout lane, and we got behind a woman who paid for thirty-two boxes of mac and cheese with change that she had to count out on the counter."

"Oh." My lips form an O and I wince. "That's painful."

"So..." His gaze drifts from Rigsby to Bella and back to me. "We missed the trip too."

"Yeah, I'm not so sure how this is going to work." I squint as I look down the road I assume my Uber took. "My ride left with my purse that had my college books, my keys, and my wallet . . ." I pause as he looks relatively unalarmed until I tack on the final item. "And your glove."

He stares forward and calmly blinks as it takes a second to register what I've said. "What?"

"I know." I shake my head, assuming he'll commiserate with me. There is no empathy infused in his tone. I honestly don't know how I'm not bawling real tears right now. It must be the shock that's holding them back. My stomach is in knots, churning with sickness.

"How could you be so careless?" It's total panic when he blurts out, "Do you understand how important that glove is? It's literally priceless. The fate of the entire AHL is riding on that glove."

I'm so taken back that my head jolts in surprise. "Me...careless?" I fumble to motion to myself with my thumb. "You lost that glove." I fight the urge to jab at his chest with my pointer finger, because he's acting so insanely rude right now. "I found your glove. Remember?"

A rumble that sounds surprisingly like the sound my dishwasher makes when it's plugged clears his throat right before he barks, "I lost it by *accident.*"

"Ope." I can't even form an actual word because this dude is so rude. I take a step back, creating some needed distance, and run my hand over the back of my neck. I get it. What I did was completely stupid, but he can't possibly know the insane amount of stress I'm under. "You think I lost it on purpose?"

"I didn't know it dropped out of my bag. You knew it was in your bag." He studies me, disbelief etched across his face. "You forgot an entire bag."

"I did." I have no problem admitting my faults. And boy, do I want to go off at the audacity of this man to insult me for not being perfect. "I momentarily forgot about it in my quest to get my daughter on the bus. I also never instructed the Uber driver to leave. That was something beyond my control."

"Oh, so you thought he'd just sit here all day waiting on your orders?" He guffaws, throwing his head back, exposing a scar under his chin. It's dark, running almost the length of his neck. It's probably from some stupid fight since he clearly has a problem with his personality. "Figures, you'd think people just do whatever you want," he mumbles under his breath. "All women are like that."

"I never said that at all, and I'd appreciate it if you didn't overload your woman issues on me."

His brow quirks, and he holds it, pausing as if he's deciding if he should argue back when I clearly know the truth. After a beat, he yanks out his phone. "I need to get a hold of that Uber driver. Did you happen to catch his name so I can request him?"

"Uh." I stare forward and refuse to answer. I don't need to be told how much I suck for not catching his name. I've had a horrible morning. I'm lucky to remember my name.

"Figures," he mutters when I don't say anything.

"Look." I hold up my phone, relieved I never stowed it in my purse. At least I have one thing to help me out. "I'll call. I can give more information."

"Suit yourself." He drops his phone to his side. For the first time since we started engaging, he looks at the boy. "I guess, we missed the bus," he explains in a much nicer tone than he used with me. "I don't know where to take you. I don't want to call your mom. I guess you can hang out with me today. I have practice in about an hour."

I tune him out because I'm connected with someone with Uber. I take a minute to explain my situation. They locate the driver who gave me a ride. I hang up and blurt out, "My Uber is currently parked downtown in front of the barber shop. He can't leave because he's been paid to wait for Mrs. Blanchard to get her hair cut, but we can run over there." I drop my gaze to the ground before I mumble, "If you want to give us a ride over there. That might be the quickest way to fix this." I hate asking for favors,

COME AND GET YOUR GLOVE

especially from Mr. Perfect, but it's freezing out, and I don't want to walk all the way down there, even if I had the time to waste.

"What are we waiting for?" He jerks his head toward the door, and I turn my gaze to Bella.

"See, this isn't going to be so bad." I put on the phony smile I'm getting so good at. "Can you hop in the back with Rick?"

"Rigsby," Bella mumbles as her feet slide forward until we reach the car. I help her in the back seat. One thing about my life is that I never need to look for an opportunity to be humbled. Nope.

I have plenty of those.

Of all the days to not have my car.

I steel my face, sealing off all my anxieties, and take the passenger seat. I have no desire to make small talk with this jerk, so I tuck my chin down and stare out my window. Thankfully, it only takes a few minutes, and we arrive at the barbershop. I easily spot my Uber and point. "There it is!"

Jackson pulls up into the empty spot right behind it, and we both push open our doors so quickly, we practically tumble out of the car. I wave wildly at the driver as I approach his car and open the back door, and blurt out apologies, "I'm so sorry for bothering you." My eyes land on a couple of bags, exactly where I had left them. One is Bella's backpack, but the other one is not mine . . . "What is this?"

My heart drums against my ribcage. All background noise fades as I deadpan on the bag that isn't mine.

It's a black purse.

Not my black purse.

I slide into the seat, put my hand on the bag, and repeat, "What is this?"

"Those are your bags," the Uber driver states, his tone losing patience.

"This is my bag." I pluck Bella's backpack from the seat and shoulder it before I dare lose it again. Then I grab the purse by the strap and hold it up as evidence. "This is not my bag."

"That's not your bag?" His brows furrow. "It's not your bag," he repeats, not as a question but as a statement, as it's finally sinking in.

"Not my bag," I say again. "Who else was in your car?" My brain is working fast, trying to solve this mystery. "Someone took my bag instead of their purse."

"Oh dear." His palm slaps his forehead. "I'm afraid that's Mrs. Wagner's purse."

"Okay." I take a deep breath and fight to keep my voice even. "Where did you take Mrs. Wagner?"

"I took her to work at the bank. She doesn't drive anymore since she has cataracts."

"The cataracts might explain how she took the wrong bag," I murmur to myself as I try to figure out the logistics. I blurt out, "I need to get to the bank, but I'm out of time." I back out of the Uber, close the door, and yell in, "Thank you!" Then I snap my gaze back to Jackson and repeat, "The bank."

He winces hard and sucks in a deep breath while he checks his watch. "I'm cutting it so close to practice. Can you grab it?"

"Me?" I'm reminded that I have an exam to take, and I'm also cutting it close. "I have a test I can't miss, or it will ruin my whole semester. I'm so close to graduating. I need a little over an hour. I can meet up with you after my class to grab it from you."

"You're not grabbing it from me, because I can't go right now," he says decisively as he crosses his arms over his chest.

"It's just practice for you. It's not like a game." I gesture forward as I'm not understanding what the big deal is. If this glove is so important, he can grab it and be a few minutes late to practice.

"You don't understand my boss. He has this whole rivalry thing. This is probably one of the most important practices of my career. If I'm even a few minutes late for practice, my boss will see it as a rebellion, and I might be thrown off the team. Not to mention this is your fault for losing the bag. You're the one who is putting me out."

"Excuse me?" I fake cough to cover all the choice words I would love to say right now, but with kids in tow, I would never lose my cool. "Putting you out?" I raise a sharp eyebrow and tack on, "Remember, I found your glove."

He childishly rolls his eyes, checks his watch again, and says, "We are wasting time."

"You're right about wasting time. Hopefully, my car will be done by then. I'll have to grab that, and I still think you might be faster to meet up with her because you have a car. To be safe, do you want to hold on to this bag, just in case you get there first. I just don't see me walking all the way down here going that fast." He takes the bag, keeping his lip buttoned. I straighten my spine, almost clicking my heels together as I peer down at Bella. I have nowhere to take her since she missed the bus. Even if I had a place, I would not have time to drop her off anywhere. "We'd better get moving. It's going to take a while to walk back to campus."

"You're going to walk all the way down there?" Jackson's lips twist with a skeptical slant. "Then you'll for sure be late. Do you want me to give you a ride?"

I'm not a prideful person, but something about the way he looks down at me with disdain makes me stand even taller. I'm done owing any man favors. "I think we can both agree that neither one of us wants to ride in a car together. I'm fine walking." I pull out my phone, open the contacts, and slide it over to him, "Can you add your phone number?"

"I'm so glad you're finally being reasonable," he mumbles but takes my phone, inserting his number before handing it back to me.

"Bye." I shove my phone in my oversized coat pocket and snatch Bella's hand while lightly pulling her forward in the opposite direction. "We need to hurry as fast as we can. My teacher is a total old hag with a miserable life who hates me."

My gut fires knots as we race down the sidewalk. Bella looks at me quizzically. "Why didn't you take the ride, Mom?"

"It's just..." I close my mouth, and fumble for words. How do I admit it is not an ego thing? I didn't like his vibe. After all the years of overlooking Chase's rude behavior, I have zero tolerance for rudeness. "It's fine," I assert as I check the time on my phone and see we are cutting it very close. I hope my teacher didn't have a horrible morning like I did, or she's not going to tolerate me arriving late. Since I can get my test done within the hour, I should be okay.

I hope.

Six

JACKSON

"Aright, Rigsby," I hustle through the arena doors, encouraging him to walk a bit faster by holding him by his sleeve. "I'm going to need you to find a seat, and you have to be quiet. I know I don't have anything to worry about with you because you will behave. Just in case, let's go over a few rules. No leaving your seat."

His eyes widen with concern as they laser up at me. "What if I have to go to the bathroom?"

"Well, if it's possible for you to hold it, I'd rather you wait. I don't want you getting lost or wandering around unsupervised."

"Got it. Pee my pants."

"No, that's not what I said." I block out the mental image he's just given me. Kids can be so gross. "I don't feel right if you're somewhere I can't see you."

"Okay." He slides his backpack from his shoulders and hooks it on his arm, pulling it forward, but it makes a thud sound.

I give his bag sideways stare. "What was that noise?"

His reply is quick. "I brought my iPad. I thought it might be something to do."

It didn't sound like any iPad I've ever heard, but I really don't have time to look at it now. If his iPad keeps him sitting still during practice, I'll take it. "Good idea." I take a deep breath as we round the corner, entering the arena. I walk to the row directly behind our penalty box and hold my arm out to usher him to a seat. "You can sit here. Don't talk. We aren't supposed to have visitors at practice. I basically need you to act like you aren't even here."

Dragging his feet at the slowest possible speed, he crosses in front of the seats and plops down. He's quiet as he stares forward, seeming to understand his assignment. "Any questions?" I ask, tilting my head down to make sure I capture any confusion in his expression.

"I got it." He nods confidently, and I take a step back with my eyes still glued to him. Nothing about this feels like it's going to have a good outcome. *I don't have a choice.* When I'm confident he's going to stay in his seat, I spin on my heel and race to the locker room. My stomach is looped into knots, but I'm going to push through it.

It's just one practice.

How bad can it be?

And please, don't let this be the day that Bill Baker shows up for practice.

Running my finger along the edge of my skate blade, I double check it before I slip it on. The guys are huge prankers. Any chance they get, they will add clear tape to someone's blade. I hope everyone is on their best behavior this week, because Bill made it clear he's watching.

Even so, I don't trust these guys.

I'm not taking chances with my gear. I can't afford any mishaps without my lucky glove. My blade is clean, and I drop my skate to the ground and slip my foot inside to begin the process of lacing it up. Tension pools in the back of my neck, making me strain to look down. I usually handle stress well, but this morning was a nightmare.

I can't even think about the fact that I still don't have my lucky glove. I pray it's at that bank when I get done with practice. Resisting the urge to shake my head, I ruminate on how that woman carelessly left her bags in an Uber. My flabbers are seriously gasted over this whole incident.

"You coming?" I look up and find Axl's foot propping the locker room door open, his gaze zeroed in on me.

I quickly scan the room—all the guys are gone. I was so zoned out that I didn't notice. "I was double-checking my gear," I mutter under my breath as I stand and lumber toward him. "Besides, we can't all be overachievers. Someone has to keep us average."

"Thanks for keeping us average." Axl chuckles, but as we move through the tunnel, we both get quiet. I haven't seen Bill, but he could seriously be lurking around any corner.

It sounds extreme.

It's not extreme for him.

"Guys, this isn't the day to slack," Coach Carlson calls from up ahead as he jerks his thumb over his shoulder. "Get on the ice."

Rolling my bottom lip under my teeth, I bite down. I'm not one to mouth off. That's Axl. He's more than earned that title for our team. I'm the quiet one who knows my place is in the net. I bob my head toward our coach and hustle forward, sighing a breath of relief when my skates finally meet the ice. My mind clicks into focus, and I take my spot in the crease and start my ritualistic procedure of skating back and forth to scuff the ice.

My gaze slides to the stands to find Rigsby. Thankfully, he's right where I left him. He smiles at me, beaming that one-front-tooth smile he's been rocking for weeks.

As I turn my head back, my neck feels even stiffer. My whole body wears a new tension. I have to believe it's because I'm worried about my glove. I don't know what else it would be. The guys are done stretching, and Coach has instructed them to run through some plays. I slide into position and watch the puck as they bring it down the ice.

Everyone seems to be skating in slow motion today. Maybe they are also on edge, but I never lose sight of the puck. I'm more than ready when Axl skates in, flicks his wrist, and slams the puck toward me.

I kick my pad out and brace for the thud. Everything goes quiet. Blinking, I check behind me.

The puck hit the net.

That was about the easiest save ever, and I let it slip past me. I roll my neck, hoping to loosen something up. I can't shake this feeling like there's something pressing on my shoulders. I never get this stressed out.

I take a deep breath, pulling in as much air as possible, and slowly let it out. The guys are in play again. I track the puck as they skate toward me again. This time I'm not going to miss an easy block. I ready my stick into position and will my eyes not to blink.

My mouth is dryer than normal, because I didn't have proper time to hydrate this morning. I run my tongue along my bottom lip. A strange sour taste lingers on my tongue, grating on my nerves a little. I do my best to ignore it. I bend my knees and laser in on the puck as Axl brings it down the ice. There's no way I will miss this shot.

Errt! Bang! Clang!

A whistle slices through the cacophony of sounds, and Coach shouts, "Who brought a kid and a giant rat to practice?"

My head whips to the sound. Sure enough, Rigsby is trotting after a tawny streak up the stairs. Behind them is a tipped over garbage can and a trail of the garbage. The streak is too big to be a rat. I have no idea what that animal is, but now Rigsby's heavy backpack makes so much sense. I swallow hard, half amazed he got it by me this whole time, and half horrified.

"One of you brought a kid and a cat," Coach hollers when nobody fesses up. "Get them out of here!"

Resisting the urge to groan, I skate forward. Coach isn't one to accept excuses or even apologies. He wants our actions to correct our mistakes, and I know nothing I say will smooth this over.

"This's your kid?" His piercing gaze lasers through me, and heat rises over my neck and ears. It's an odd way to show embarrassment, but it's how I've always been.

"My sister's. I'm babysitting while she has a baby today. He missed the school bus. Sorry, I don't have anywhere to take him." I skate around the rink and exit the ice. I can feel everyone's eyes on me as I lumber forward because I'm still in my skates. I'm trying to balance on the concrete as I'm about to whisper-yell at Rigsby, but I freeze before I get a word out. He's crawling over the seats to catch his cat-rat. It's clearly a game to the creature. I'm going to have to help him catch it, and I can't do anything with skates on.

With a heavy huff, I lean over, unlace my skates, slip my feet out, and start the process of climbing the stairs after them, which is nearly impossible to do with goalie gear on. I drop my helmet right as the creature sees me. Arching his back as if he's getting ready to challenge me, he takes off, hopping from the back of one seat to the next like he's spring loaded. He's flying! Now that I'm closer I can tell it's not a cat or a rat. It's a ferret!

Aw man, Jackie never told me he got a ferret. She's going to owe me so big for this. I run at top speed, leaping over chairs. Rigsby lunges forward, narrowly missing the ferret. I race to the top to try to get him from that angle. He's a ninja ferret who drops to the ground and darts under the seats. Apparently, he has invisibility powers now, because I can't see even a streak.

I stop, resting my hands on my knees as I catch my breath and scan the arena. I get a glimpse of the ferret's long body all the way down on the ground floor. How he traveled that far in such a short amount of time is beyond me. *He's sprinting to the exit!*

The sharp blast from the whistle slices through the air as Coach shouts even louder, "Practice isn't starting back up until that kid and rat are gone!"

A collective groan rises from the team. A few of the guys skate off the ice and start toward me, joining in the search. That's great and all, but my fingers are trembling. Coach Carlson is not going to forgive this very easily. He's not a guy with a sense of humor.

Not this week.

Not ever.

In hindsight, I should have called Jackie when we missed the school bus. She's in labor but she might have had a babysitter I could have called.

I take a deep swallow and get a gulp of air that tastes a little like the perfect blend of failure and frustration. Then I run as fast as I can out the door, trailing that animal.

With a deep scowl on my face, I trudge out of practice.

I've never done this before. I can't even begin to imagine all the ways I'll be punished when I return, but I don't have a choice.

With the not-happy ferret jailed in the backpack, and Rigsby snatched by the wrist, I scurry out of the arena. My head is pounding after all that commotion. I still can't believe we caught this ninja ferret. He ended up running into an open supply closet where we surrounded him. I've never seen Carlson's face turn a deeper shade of red than when he screamed for me to get the animal out of there.

I guess I'll go back to my apartment and figure something out. I have a press conference this afternoon, and I don't dare bring Rigsby to that. The last thing I need is this chaos captured on camera.

Breathing heavily, I propel Rigsby forward, and he trips over his foot trying to keep up with me. What stands out the most in my mind is how I completely missed an entire ferret. The kid is either a genius or I'm losing my mind. I let him into the backseat of my car, drop his bag into his hands, promptly get in the front seat, and take a moment to catch my breath. "Hey, buddy," I proceed in my best gentle coax, "how'd you sneak a ferret into the arena? Better yet," I rush as my mind reels, "where has he been this whole time?"

"Simple." Unamused, his bottom lip pushes out. "He lives in my backpack."

"But—" I drop it because it really is exactly the opposite of how he described it. It's a giant feat to conceal a pet, and I'm quite impressed. I study his expression in the rearview mirror. Now that the ferrets out-of-the-bag—literally and figuratively—he opens the top of his bag. The ferret melts into his arms, rolling on his back for a belly scratch. "So, how long have you had him?"

"Since the beginning of last summer. He was our class pet last year. The teacher had to give him a summer home, so I volunteered." A proud smile curves on the corner of his lips as he continues to rub his pet.

"So . . . your mom doesn't know?"

"Nah, I wanted to tell her, but she's doesn't really like pets. She was pregnant all summer and not in the best mood. I figured what she doesn't know can't hurt her, right?" He meets my gaze in the mirror and pinches his lips together. "I guess you're going to tell her."

Aside from the whole almost getting me fired thing, it's kind of funny, but I don't think it's my place to encourage dishonesty. "You know," I start, but then stop as I realize this is going to come off as scolding. If he can keep a pet alive and a secret for four months, maybe he deserves to keep it. "Well, maybe I'll convince her to let you keep it."

His eyebrows rise, as his pupils widen with hope, and I tack on, "As long as you swear to never bring him into a hockey arena again."

He dips his face to speak to the ferret, "Hear that, Frankfurter? No more hockey."

"You named him after a hotdog?"

"No," he speaks with all the seriousness a seven-year-old can muster. "No, not a hotdog. His name is Frank Fur, as in he has fur, and Ter as in more."

"Oh." Now that that's settled, I give the back of my head a healthy scratch and check my phone for any messages from Kaci.

Nothing. I was hoping she would get done with her test early.

Apparently, she's not in a hurry to retrieve her things or my glove. How irresponsible can someone be? I guess I'll take care of it.

I crank the engine and shift it into gear, calling back, "We have to stop at the bank, and then we can grab lunch." As I take a left turn out of the parking lot, I whisper under my breath, "Let's hope nothing else goes wrong today."

Seven

KACI

"Alright, baby." I exhale in uneven bursts as we climb the stairs to the second-floor classroom. Struggling to feel my fingers, I curl them into tight fists. That jog to campus was a little too cold and a little too far. "I can't afford to take you to the drop-in day care today. Not to mention I don't have the time or a car. I need you to be the quietest you've ever been." I hand her my phone, which is open to her favorite YouTube channel and point to the wall outside my classroom. I hate leaving her here, but there's no way I can bring her inside the classroom. "Do not go anywhere," I give her the sternest warning. "Don't talk to anyone, and I'll be as fast as I can." Guilt floods my chest, tightly cinching my lungs.

What am I doing?

I can't even think clearly, as my heart is pounding so fast.

I can't miss this test.

She's going to be fine.

Mapleton is safe, and I'm right inside the classroom door that's open.

I've got this.

I release a breath and smile at her. She's already scrolling for a video with Little B tucked safely to her side. I slip inside the classroom door. Thankfully, everyone who gets here early fills the back rows first, and I take the corner seat in the front row. If I lean to the left, I can see Bella's shoes peeking from around the edge of the doorframe.

Tapping my foot against my desk leg, I stare ahead at Bella's foot while the professor walks around the room, handing out the tests. A quick glance at my desk sends me into a jolt of panic—it's completely bare. *I don't even have a pencil to write with.*

What a nightmare.

I peek at the woman sitting next to me. Dressed in head-to-toe lounge wear, and she slouches down in her seat, as if she doesn't have a care in the world. For the briefest of moments, I envy how relaxed she appears on this test day. Meanwhile, I'm perched on the edge of my seat, my heart refusing to slow. Leaning over, I hiss, "Hey, I'm sorry to bug you, but I lost my purse. Can I borrow a pencil?"

Her gaze slides over to me, and her lips remained pressed in an unengaged line. After a beat of silence, I whisper a little louder, "Hey, can I borrow a pencil?"

"Ladies," the professor's stern warning slices through the air. "Tests are out. There is no talking."

My bottom jaw drops open in helplessness. With no other options, I'm forced to speak directly to the professor. "I'm sorry, but my car broke this morning. I grabbed an Uber. In the bustle of trying to get my daughter to school, I forgot my bag in the Uber. I don't have a pencil. Is there any way I can borrow one?"

My white-haired professor stares over the rims of her glasses with an angled glare, one that has the power to make the hairs on the back of my neck stand up straight. "Are you saying you came to class unprepared?"

"Uh, yes." I gulp. While still making eye contact with my professor, a woman sitting behind me taps my shoulder with a pen. My heart literally does a backflip. I grab the pen and hold onto it with a death grip, wishing I could make myself smaller. I hate this feeling of inferiority.

It's not just this test.

Every day, I walk through life, and I feel like I'm one of those people stuck on the bottom rung of society. It's in the way people look at me when I pull into the parking lot with a car that has a mismatched door, or when I pay at the grocery store, counting out the single dollars I earned from tips.

If I'm honest, that's the reason I'm in this seat. I'm doing my best to level up this life. In my daydreams, I imagine graduation, and how it will feel to quit my job at the restaurant. My goal is to come back someday as a customer and leave the staff the biggest tips of their lives—

My daydream is cut short by the professor handing me the test. It's thick—easily eight to ten pages—and my heart sinks.

This is going to take all day.

I flip through the pages, finding most of them are multiple choice, and sit back, waiting for the professor to begin the listening portion of the test. As a music major, we always start each test with an exercise where a random part of a composition we studied is played. We have about ten seconds to identify the song and composer and write it down.

I hate this part.

I'm not one of those gifted people who can play by ear or identify things quickly. I ready my pen, and focus my attention as the professor starts the first composition. It's quiet, and I can barely hear it, even when I strain my ear in that direction. I have no idea what it is, but I write something down.

The next song plays, and it's loud, with thundering drums that rumble the floor of the classroom. Out of the corner of my eye, I catch Bella on her feet, doing ballet leaps through the hall to the pounding beat. My face scrunches into a wince as I lean over, trying to get her attention. Her face is lit up with the brightest smile. I get that she's happy, but she needs to sit still and not draw attention to herself. "Bella," I whisper-shout.

"Miss Roberts." My professor turns on her heel with a pointed glare. "I'm not going to tell you again that the tests are out. No talking. Another peep from you, and your test will be removed from your hands, and you'll receive a zero."

"Yes, ma'am," I mutter under my breath and drop my gaze to my test. She starts another recording, and I almost gasp because I know this one. I quickly jot down the title, and in the background, I hear Bella say, "Hello?"

My ears perk as my attention floats back to the door. She goes on to say, "Nope. I'm with my mom at school, because she's too poor to take me to day care."

My jaw drops, and my cheeks fire. She must have answered my phone. I wonder who called? It doesn't sound like she's talking to my mom. What if it's the school!? I didn't even think to call in her absence because everything was crazy. I struggle not to shout toward the door for her to be quiet. I don't want to get my test taken away, but she goes on. "Aw, I'm not sure when she's going to be done. Her teacher's an old hag with a miserable life, and she hates my mom."

I can feel them. Everyone's eyes are on me. I dare to glance at my professor, and she's glaring, her nostrils flaring.

That's it. I'm totally cooked.

I drop my borrowed pen to my desk, stand, and take my walk of shame toward the door.

There's no point in trying to finish this test, my hag-of-a-teacher is going to fail me after she hears that. As I flee, my shoes click against the tile floor, drawing more attention than I can handle. Once outside the door, tears prick the backs of my eyes. I hold my palm out, signaling for Bella to give me the phone. "Hang up the phone," I whisper harshly.

A group of students meander past, all their eyes seeming to linger on me. Suddenly, I'm aware of how this looks. I force a toothy smile on my face and repeat in a softer tone, "Baby, give me the phone."

"One moment, she wants to talk to you," Bella states as she hands the phone over.

"Is it the school?" I mouth, but she just pushes the phone toward me.

Taking it, I check over my shoulder, walk a few steps from the open classroom door, and whisper into the phone, "Hello."

"Kaci," a deep voice flows into my ear. "It's Jackson."

My head springs back, and I stand up straight, "Uh, okay. I'm taking a test. Is this an emergency?"

"I went to the bank to get our things, but Mrs. Wagner had left work early. I just missed her."

"She did?" My breath blows out in one long even exhale. The tears I've been holding back get heavier, weighing on the backs of my eyes. This nightmare is just getting worse. "Did they say where she went?"

"Yeah, she went to lunch at Red Barn. One of her coworkers called her cell phone, and I got to talk to her. She said she hadn't even noticed her bag was different."

"Oh, really." I feel my face scrunch in total disbelief as I can't fathom how someone could not notice that.

"She's waiting for me. I'll take Rigsby over there for food, and then exchange the bags. Did you want to meet me there?"

"Well, I don't have my car yet, and it will take a while for us to walk down there." I blink, pushing back my tears. This entire day has left me feeling so vulnerable.

"Don't worry about it," he says. "I don't want to miss her. I'll just run down there and take care of it. If you can make it before we leave, that's fine. If not, I'll give you a call."

"Okay." I force the tears out of my voice and agree since that sounds like a reasonable plan. Afterall, I must finish my test—*Oh no*! I drop my phone to my side and pivot toward the door. My professor is standing directly in front of it with one hand on her hip, glaring over her nose at me.

"Are you done, Miss Roberts?"

"Yes, ma'am. I'm s-sorry," I stutter, and click my heels together as if I'm in some weird military establishment. It's an odd reaction, but she gives me that vibe.

"You left the room during an exam to talk on the phone. I have to assume the worst, and that you were looking up answers." She holds up a bundle of papers, which I quickly recognize as my test, and proceeds to slowly rip it in half from top to bottom.

I have no words.

I get it.

I can't resume my test after being in the hall on the phone. It looks shady, but if only I could make her understand how important this is to me. I didn't choose for my morning to implode. "I'm sorry," I mouth, my voice cracking into an audible sound at the end. "Any chance I can get a retake?"

"Not a chance." She points down the hall toward the staircase that leads to the exit. "You're done here, and this is a final warning. You are welcome back to class but let this be a lesson. I have thirty other students in this class, all of whom paid thousands of dollars to be here. It's not fair to them if you are disruptive during this time."

"I'm sorry." It comes out sounding more like a question. By some miracle I manage to hold my tears until she's disappeared inside the room.

"Mama," Bella says, her glistening eyes staring up at me. "You're crying."

I try my best to blink the tears away so I can blame it on an eyelash, but they only fall harder.

I'm forced to let her see me fail.

This isn't the role model I wanted to be for her.

"I, uh, just have something in my eye," I finally manage to say. "But the good news is I'm done with class." I force a small smile, the only one I have left. "And that man on the phone was Jackson. He said to meet him downtown at Red Barn for my bag."

"Oh." Her eyes immediately widen. "Are we eating there?"

It's not a place I frequent because it's expensive. Frankly, on my budget, we never eat out anywhere. After the morning we've had, it feels right to make an exception to bring a little light into our day. "If I get my purse back, and the money is still in it, we can share a burger."

"Yay, Mom." She rushes toward the steps, leading the way back down. "I get the bigger half."

I doubt I can even eat. My stomach is one giant ball of knots, and I force my feet to carry me from my classroom. I just started my semester off with a big fat zero, and I resist the urge to hang my head.

I did the best I could.

I have three more exams this semester. I'll have to get As on the rest to raise my average, or I'll fail. Sure, I can retake the class, but this is supposed to be my last semester, which means more money for the class and another semester of living in a dump, driving a car whose only reliability is breaking down.

I'm tired of being broke.

I'm ready for a new life.

Eight

JACKSON

"I think that's her." I gesture toward the lady wearing a red-feather hat in the back booth. She's an elegant woman, sitting tall with her shoulders back and conversing with a group of friends.

I arch my neck, doing a double take to make sure, and my stomach churns. A rich, smoky aroma with hints of spices and tangy undertones invite me farther inside. I step, but the hostess stops me. With her hair up in one of those high cheerleader ponytails, she eyes Mrs. Wagner's purse that I'm holding. It's an uncomfortable moment as I'm feeling completely awkward carrying this impossible-to-miss black bag, which isn't even remotely a tad masculine with its gold hardware and flower-embossed leather. I shift the bag to my other arm and tuck it like it's a football. "Hey," I upnod, "how's it going?"

"Back again?" She gives me a sly smile.

It takes me a second to realize it's the same hostess who seated us last night. "Yeah, just us again." My gaze slides to Rigsby, who is eyeing the long list of signature barbeque sauces they have displayed on their wall. It's one of the many things they are famous for. I motion to the row labeled "Melt Your Face Heat Level." There are crying and sweating emojis next to it. I've always loved spicy food, and this is the row I order from. "What do you think, bud? Do you want to try a little Inferno Fire today?"

"I'm going with just ketchup this time." He steps forward, and we follow the hostess to a booth near the front windows. She offers each of us a menu and strides away.

I plant my palms on the table and say, "You stay right here." I pause, checking to make sure he doesn't have his backpack with him. No mystery pets should be escaping. We had ran back to my apartment and locked Frankfurtor in my bedroom, and I pray that's where he stays. "I'm going to talk to that woman quickly. If the waitress comes, order me a water."

He agrees, and I hurry over with the purse in my hand. "Mrs. Wagner," I rush out, my breathing coming out in heavy gasps. "I have your purse."

She turns to me, and the moment her eyes land on me, her face brightens with a welcoming smile. "Well, hello there."

"Nice to meet you." I nod at her dinner companions and hold the purse up to her eye level. I have no interest in wasting time on pleasantries. I desperately need to make sure she has my glove. "Here's your bag." I thrust it toward her, not hesitating a second to ask, "Do you still have Kaci's bag?"

"I do." She shakes her head, a foolish chuckle escaping out of her lips. "I have no idea how this mix-up happened, but I'm sure glad it got fixed before I even realized there was a problem."

"Right." I clench my teeth, realizing she's content to drag out this interaction.

"And you are the sweetest gentleman for making sure my purse was returned." She gives me a tilt of her head while her smile lingers.

"Uh, you're welcome." I shift my weight from my left foot to my right and casually lean over the side of the table to see if Kaci's bag is on the other side of the booth.

I don't see it at all.

This could be bad.

What if she lost it? My heartbeat ramps up, and I ask again, "Do you have the other purse?"

"I do." Her chin dips into a deep nod, but she still doesn't move to gather it.

"Can I have it?" My words are slow at first, but then I rush to add, "I don't mean to be rude, but I'm babysitting my nephew. He's sitting all alone at that table, and I need to get back to him."

"Oh." She peruses the tables until she spots Rigsby, and she finally reaches under the table and pulls out an over-sized black purse. It's zipped up tight at the top. I can't tell if my glove is in it, but it's awfully full of something. "Here you go." She extends the bag to me, and I quickly take it. The bag slams to the ground. It's so heavy it feels like bricks are in it. How she didn't wonder about the weight when she grabbed the wrong one is beyond me.

"Thanks so much." I back away from the table, tossing up a hand in a quick wave goodbye before pivoting and unzipping the bag as I hurry back to my booth.

It's the moment of truth.

So much is riding on this reveal.

Is my glove here?

The zipper pulls hard and gets caught on something.

I tug, but it still won't budge.

Do I feel bad busting in Kaci's purse?

No, not at all, because I rescued it for her.

When I reach the table, I plop the bag down, adjust my grip, and yank on the zipper with all my might—and it releases, snapping the zipper off the track. I can see inside the bag and my glove is. . . in it!

A cold sheen of sweat dots my brow. I snatch the glove from the bag, place the bag next to me on the booth, and drop down to sit, practically cradling the glove in my hands.

Not going to lie.

If I wasn't in public, I might kiss it.

"There you are," a frantic female voice spats from behind me. I turn my head the slightest. Kaci is tugging her daughter in the same manner I've been tugging Rigsby along all morning.

With triumph, I snatch her purse handle and hold it up. "Got it!"

Her free hand flies to cover her heart, and her eyelashes flutter as if she's blinking back tears. "What a relief." Her words come out with a deep exhalation.

I hand the purse over and take note of how her eyes snag on the broken zipper. Feeling bad I broke it, even though it was an accident, I offer her an apologetic smile. "I had an accident opening it to get my glove, but I promise I didn't take anything. It only looks like you were mugged."

"Ah." Her fingers rub the split seam that leaves a gaping hole. "I don't even care about this. My whole life is in the bag." Her hand dives in and rummages around as she inventories her things. When she's content with what she sees, her gaze slopes back at me. "Thank you for grabbing it."

"Yeah, you bet." I flick my hand in a dismissive gesture, as if this was the easiest thing in the world to do in the middle of my workday.

The waitress returns and pushes a menu toward Kaci's hand. "Are you joining this table? If you would like your own, I can add you to the waitlist. It's about twenty minutes."

"Oh, a twenty-minute wait." She twists her wrist to look at her watch, and frowns while she turns to Bella. "Baby, I don't know if we have time to eat. I have to get to that funeral."

Bella's face reflects disappointment, and before I can stop myself, I blurt out, "You can join us."

Why did I do that?

It's the people pleaser in me, and the fact that I can't stand to see a hungry kid. Kaci's stress is evident in the lines of her forehead. She looks exactly how I feel. Like I deserve a nice meal and a moment to sit down.

"Nah." Kaci's foot slides back as if she's physically rejecting the invitation, but Bella's face pales. I get what she's feeling. I would be devastated if I was standing in the middle of a barbeque restaurant and didn't get to stay for even an appetizer.

Rigsby waves his hand over the table to show our lack of drinks. "We haven't even ordered yet. It's perfect timing, and Bella's hungry."

Bella's already climbing in, and Kaci flashes me a hesitant smile. "If you really don't mind, we're both starving and so pressed for time. I have a funeral and..." her voice drops off as her gaze latches on to Bella, and she adds, "If I can even go with Bella. I'm not sure that's such a great idea. I got kicked out of my test because of the distraction."

"Sounds like my morning." I pause and ponder how to speak in code. I hate to speak negatively about Rigsby in front of him, but my morning was a disaster. "I got kicked out of my practice because of my distraction."

Kaci tips her head to the side before she levels her gaze on me with a bit of a pointed glare. "That sounds awful. I know you think this is on the same level of atrocity, but it really, *really* isn't." Her words are slow, as if she's weighing each one very carefully. "I got a *zero* on a test because of *you*. Not because of my child, but because of you calling me. You knew I was in class. Do you understand what that does to my grade?"

I blink and slide to the edge of my seat, emotion budding in my chest. It's not anger, but confusion. How is this my fault? "Why did you answer it?"

"I didn't know who it was. I thought it was an emergency with the school since I never called to let them know Bella was absent. I didn't want them to report her missing or call the cops or something." She isn't unkind in her tone, but there's an edge, warning me that she's not one to be pushed over. Though that wasn't what I was trying to do. She sure knows how to speak up for herself. Feisty.

"Ah, I guess I clearly wasn't thinking." Raking my hand through my hair, I take a deep breath. "I've been doing this parenting thing for one day, and I'm just frazzled. I wasn't trying to get you in trouble. To be honest, I never went to college. It didn't dawn on me that you could get a zero for that. I'm sorry."

Her gaze remains unwavering, as if she is studying my every twitch. I run my hand through my hair again. *Maybe inviting her to eat wasn't a great idea? Not if she's going to glare at me the whole time.* I attempt to glare back, but her bright eyes spiral all the light back at me. They aren't frightening or even that effective for glaring. It's like when a poodle attempts to growl. You can't help but laugh because they think they are tough, but they are the only ones. I guess if anyone is going to glare at me, it might as well be someone with a gorgeous face like hers.

The waitress walks up, taking a moment to smile at everyone. "Did you have time to look at the menu? I'm happy to answer any questions."

"I'm good." I look at Kaci, and she nods, so I order. "We'll have a couple of root beers, and the bucket of boneless wings—one half Fire Inferno and the other half plain with about five sides of ketchup."

The waitress jots down the order and then looks at Kaci. "And for you, ma'am?"

"We're going to share a cheeseburger with a side of fries and two glasses of water, please."

"Sounds good." The waitress gathers our menus and points to the tablet on the table. "If you need to add anything to your order, you can do so on that tablet, and there are also games for the kids."

That catches the attention of both kids. Rigsby snatches the tablet, but I place my hand on top of it and caution, "Only if you share."

"And you put it away as soon as the food comes," Kaci tacks on. Rigsby has already decided to crawl under the table. He pops up on the other side, squeezing between Bella and Kaci to get a better view of the tablet.

"That was easy." I never cease to be amazed by Rigsby's lack of shyness. I raise my hand and rub my temples, my brain throbbing. I can't believe how badly this morning went. If I don't find something to do with Rigsby for my press conference, I'll likely be benched for the next game—if I keep my position. I need a babysitter. Someone who can watch him for an hour or so. I let out a heavy sigh and stare across the table.

Kaci's peering at the tablet, making sure the kids are taking turns. She's not my favorite person on the planet, but she's in the same position . . . and a solution pops into my head. I lean forward. "Hey, I have an idea."

"Oh, yeah. What's that?" She barely glances at me, just sweeping her lashes up for a mere second before bringing her focus back to the tablet.

"I'm sorry about this morning. As I said, I wasn't thinking," I swallow, as I'm still hoping she'll look this way. She seems to be doing everything she can to ignore me. I go on. "The truth is, I'm super stressed right now. My day is packed full of things, as I'm sure yours is. I was wondering if we can form a truce and team up to help each other get through our day. I can watch Bella for anything you need to get done, if you can take Rigsby for my press conference."

Her lips slowly bend into a smile as she catches up, and her gaze peels off the tablet to focus on me. "I like the idea of having some help. I can take them for your conference. I have a funeral and another class. I would love help during my class before I end up failing that one too." Her eyes widen as her hand digs into her coat pocket. She pulls out her phone and reads a text. "My car is done, and they are going to drop it off. Isn't that another relief?"

"It sounds like this day finally got better." I sigh and lean back.

"Right." The airy chuckle that slips from her lips is so cute that it causes me to look at her mouth. She really does have a beautiful smile with full pouty lips that seem to naturally pucker. Hmm. It's weird I didn't notice that before, but maybe it's because, up until now, she was mostly scowling at me.

The waitress drops off our food. I don't waste a moment digging in. My first bite is so delicious, it hits the spot, further solidifying that today is finally turning around. After taking another bite and swallowing, I can't resist saying, "I'm so glad the worst of the day is over."

Her lips pucker until they land at an impish pout. "Please don't jinx it."

"That's nonsense." I dismiss her warning with the wave of my hand and grab another wing, tearing off the breading with my teeth. This meal is heavenly. "Don't be silly," I add through my mouthful of food. "Let's be optimistic, so our luck turns around."

"I wish it was that easy." She pokes at her half of the burger, lifts the bun, and wrinkles her nose. She sets it back on her plate, ultimately sliding the shared plate to rest directly in front of Bella.

"Is something wrong with your food?" I crunch through another wing.

"Nah, nothing's wrong with it. I'm not a big beef person, especially when my stomach is nervous. I only ordered it because that's what Bella wanted. The portions are big enough for us to share a meal here, and I didn't want to pay for two meals. Not this week anyway. Not with my car breaking down and all."

My brow furrows, as it doesn't seem right that she's not eating anything. I think back to when Bella said her mom was too poor to take her to childcare. I really didn't pay much attention at the time, but I understand it's got to be rough being a single mom in this economy. I wouldn't want anyone to go hungry. I grab my bucket of wings and tilt it toward her. "Have some chicken."

"It's fine." She gingerly swats the bucket away, but I notice her gaze lingering at the wings, betraying her true desire. "I'm not going to eat your food."

"It's not a big deal. We have like forty wings." I offer her the bucket again. "You're hungry, and your car isn't here yet. You have time to eat a couple."

She slowly shifts her focus to my bucket again. "If you insist. I'll try one."

I wait for her to take one and then set the bucket down, watching as she nibbles off the edge. Her eyelashes lower, as if she's savoring each bit, and she sweetly hums, "These are good. Nice and crunchy."

"I told you that you'd like them." I can't resist a bigger smile, and I reach into the bucket again. "Take as many as you want." I'm grateful we stopped bickering, and since she's going to help me with my conference, I'm going to try to keep her happy. If food is what does the trick, then she can have it all.

"That's your food." She covers her mouth as she speaks and shakes her head.

I can eat anything—my stomach is a tank—and I hate to see her not eat until she's full. Before she has a moment to argue, I reach across the table, grab her half of the burger, and swap it for my bucket of wings. "Fair trade," I assert. "You take my chicken, and I'll eat the half of the burger that was going to go to waste."

"No, that's not fair." She tries to reach across the table, but I'm slick. I pick up her burger, lick the top of the bun, then flash a mischievous smile at her. "And my germs are all over this now, so you can't take it back."

"You really didn't have to swap food with me." Traces of humor inflections flicker in the middle of her eyes, and my ego inflates now that I've cheered her up.

"No, I did not, but it's the least I could do after I ruined your test." I take a bite of the burger and chew for a minute before I add, "Plus, you called a truce. So, we are friends now."

Her face stills as her gaze settles on mine. For the first time since we met each other, she allows herself time to hold my direct gaze. In an odd way, it's like I'm finally really meeting her. Meeting her without distractions and errands. Just her.

I can tell she has stopped resisting when she retrieves the biggest chicken wing and moves it next to her lips. Before she bites, she says, "Thank you, Jackson."

"Well, you might not be thanking me after you babysit Rigsby," I mutter under my breath. "He had a surprise ferret this morning."

A soft chuckle bleeps out of her lips, and she flashes me a pleading smile. "Well, at least I'll have a full belly to deal with the rest of this crazy day."

"So true." I take another bite of the burger and check on Rigsby. He and Bella are still playing tablet games together, exactly like they weren't supposed to once the food came, but they are both smiling and happy. I'm starting to understand why parents love these tablets. It's a moment of respite from the chaos.

I'm not taking that tablet from them.

I glance back at Kaci, who's already moved on to another chicken wing, completely lost in her enjoyment of the food.

Apparently, she needs a break from the chaos too.

Her phone dings as she finishes a third chicken wing. She reads a text and immediately opens her purse, pulling out her wallet to count dollar bills. "My car is in front. If I don't want to be late for my class, I really should leave now." She thumbs through a stack of one-dollar bills and sets them in the center of the table. "This is for our portion of the bill."

I gesture toward her money. "I've got it covered. You barely ate anything."

"Let me pay for my share since we intruded on your lunch. But if you are sure you don't mind watching Bella, I'll gladly take the free babysitting."

"I don't mind, and I'm not arguing with reciprocal free babysitting." Knowing Kaci will be watching Rigsby during my press conference takes a huge load off my shoulders.

"Thank you," she says with sincerity in her voice. "You're really saving my life here."

"Same." I nod and add, "Trust me, the pleasure is all mine."

She stands and takes a deep breath as she faces Bella. I take a moment to nonchalantly lean over, and in a clandestine move, tuck her money into her purse. It's easy to do since the zipper is broken. I get a gentle whiff of her scent—subtle and sophisticated—exactly how you think it would be for a woman as strong and beautiful as her.

"Okay, Bella," she explains to her daughter. "You're going to play with Rigsby for about an hour. I'll be right back to pick you up. Okay?"

"Bye, Mom." Bella waves without looking up from her tablet. Slouching further into the booth, I chuckle to myself about how easy this is going to be. The kids haven't diverted their attention from that tablet.

Something feels odd though.

It's almost like Kaci left a subtle trail of that delicious scent, because I could swear it lingers even though she's long gone. I look behind me, half expecting her to be standing there, but she's gone.

That's crazy.

Scratching the back of my head, I look around but still don't see her.

I do, however, spot the waitress bringing the check, which is perfect timing. I pay her directly, and since we're finished eating, we bundle up, and meander to the door. "Alright, guys." I hold the door open as they pass and step onto the downtown sidewalk. "We only have about an hour to kill before we have to meet back up with Kaci. What do you want to do?"

"How about the park?" Rigsby jumps up and down in excitement, as if I can't see him.

"Uh, it's a little cold to stand outside." I look down Main Street, scanning the little shops. "Let's see...we just ate. We don't have enough time to catch a movie. Hmm, how about the children's art museum?"

Rigsby eyes hold steady as if he's fighting an eye roll. Bella's lips curl up, and she hugs the bear she's holding tighter to her chest. "Yeah, they have an open studio during the week. My mom sometimes takes me there on days we don't have school."

"That sounds perfect for us." I extend my hand, ushering them down the sidewalk. There is no point to driving a couple of blocks when the downtown parking is limited. As usual, Mapleton is bustling with people coming in and out of the shops. We weave through the shoppers while I try to keep them both by my side. "So, Bella," I begin, glancing at her quickly before focusing back on where I'm walking. "Your mom likes art?"

"Yeah, she's a creative type." Bella pushes her hands into her puffer coat pockets. "She's the opposite of my dad."

"Oh, yeah?" My ears perk at the mention of Kaci's ex, and I'm a little curious. "What does your dad like?"

"According to my mom, he only likes himself." Pointing forward, she exclaims, "Oh, there's the museum." It's like the kids have some telepathic connection, because without saying a word, they race the rest of the block and barge through the front door without waiting for me.

"Guys!" I yell, but it's no use. The door has already closed behind them. I give up and jog to catch them.

I've never been to this children's museum before. As soon as I open the door, I'm met with so much color, it looks like a rainbow exploded on the walls. The desk attendant looks up with a cheery smile on her face. "Good morning, kids. No school today?"

"We missed the field trip bus," Rigsby says proudly. That feels like days ago, even though it's only been a few hours. It's been a long day already.

I step forward, while pulling out my wallet. "We thought there was some art studio thing they could do."

"Yeah." She nods with a happy-to-help -you smile on her face. "It's for our preschool audience, but since your kids are younger, I can sneak them in." She moves to her computer and clicks the mouse a few times. "So, just your two kids then?"

"Well, two, but they aren't mine." I slide out my debit card and pass it to her, shrugging one shoulder. "I'm babysitting."

"That works too." She takes my card and slides it through her machine. "It's twelve dollars." After the card clears, she hands it back and points down the hall to the left. "Bathrooms, lockers, and the gift shop are this way." She waves her hand down the opposite hall and says, "The art studio is all the way down this hall. You'll find aprons and everything you need inside the door."

"Thank you." I place a hand on each kid's shoulder and steer them away from the desk. They ignore me. Instead, break into a foot race. Once again, I call after them, "Guys, this is a museum. No running."

Apparently, they are situationally deaf, because they don't slow. Once again, I find myself speed-walking after them. Inside the studio, they aren't shy about making themselves at home, moving around the tables, and collecting brushes and paints for themselves.

The studio attendant shows them how to properly set up their pallet. I meander over to their workstation, prop a shoulder against the wall, and observe as the attendant proceeds to demonstrate brush strokes. My eyelids grow heavy. This has been one of the longest days I've had in a long time. "What are you painting?" I ask through a yawn.

Bella swirls her brush over her canvas while pinning her lips into a secret smile. "It's a surprise."

"Oh, I can't wait." I shift my gaze to Rigsby. "What about you, bud? Are you painting your uncle being the most amazing goalie ever?"

"Ha." He throws his head back and sputters out an exaggerated laugh. My phone vibrates from inside my coat pocket. Reaching inside, I grab it and read the text message.

Kaci: How is everything going?

Snickering, I check the time. It's been fifteen minutes, and she's already checking on me. There's no way I cannot have fun with this.

Jackson: I already lost them both.

Kaci: You're kidding.

Her response comes quickly as I expect, followed by another one that's rapidly fired.

Kaci: Be honest. I'm just getting to my class, but I'll come running if I need to.

Jackson: I'm kidding.

Jackson: You seriously only gave me fifteen minutes. What did you expect to happen?

Kaci: Hopefully nothing.

Jackson: We are fine. I'm putting my phone away. Pay attention to your class.

I watch my phone to see if she replies. I can only imagine the way she would be glaring at me if she were here. She thinks she's tough, but I might not be able to hold my expression steady. I can picture that pouty lip aimed right at me...

It's more funny than it is intimidating.

Well, funny and adorable.

I stare for another minute and get no texts.

Wow, she actually listened. Hmm. I put my phone back in my pocket and casually look at the kids, and I jolt.

They swirl their hands through giant circles of paint spread across the table, giggling uncontrollably. Their protective aprons are useless—I can barely see them beneath the smears and handprints they've stamped all over each other. "Guys!" I lunge forward and then pause, not sure what I'm going to do. I'm not touching this mess. "Stop it," I scold and take a cautious step closer, scanning the room for the attendant. Apparently, she's stepped out.

"We are murals." Rigsby turns to me, and I bust out laughing. He has a blue mustache painted above his upper lip. Aside from the mess, it's pretty on-character. I shift my attention to Bella. Sure enough, she's also in character with yellow over her lip and red to her cheeks.

I jab my hand through my hair as the tension piles into my shoulder. It's sort of funny, and I can't even be mad at them. I took my eyes off them for just two minutes. Now I have to get them cleaned up before Kaci freaks out, and blames me for not watching them. I don't have time to run home, and Rigsby doesn't have another change of clothes anyway.

An idea pops into my head. "Guys," I raise my voice, "Painting class is over. We need to go shopping."

Nine

KACI

With a renewed appreciation for personal car ownership and no longer caring that one of my car doors doesn't match the others, I proudly park in the only empty spot on the block. It happens to be right outside the general store, the place Jackson said to meet him. It's a good thing too, because I need a new purse. I keep forgetting the zipper on mine is broken. Twice it has tipped over and things have fallen out. The last thing I need today is to lose my wallet. Instead of taking my purse, I grab only my wallet and go inside.

Jackson is right where he said they would be—up front by the candy machines. From the size of the smiles on the kids' faces, they've had more than I would have given them. I stride through the door and greet Bella with a smile. "Hey, honey."

She's holding Little B, which is exactly what I expect. When she turns to me, I'm a bit jarred to see her cheeks painted red and a mustache under her nose. I leak out a chuckle. "It looks like you had fun."

"I turned my attention away for a minute to text you, and that's what happened." Jackson steps closer to me, a wry smile on his face. "Not to mention their shirts were ruined. I brought them here for new ones. I hope it's okay, but I threw the one she had in the trash. It wasn't worth saving."

My gaze travels down Bella's outfit. Her jacket is unzipped, revealing a navy shirt peeking out instead of the one she was wearing before. "You didn't have to pay for new clothes."

"If you had seen them, you would say something different." His words braid with a light-hearted chuckle, as the kids beam. A weird feeling washes over me. Like I missed out on a party or something.

"Well, that's nice of you, but not expected. How much was it?" Still holding my wallet, I start to unzip it. "I'll pay you back."

"You don't owe me anything." He places his hand over mine, and an electric zap rockets through my arm. We both freeze, our eyes locking instantly. I want to ask, *what was that*!? I can see by the way his eyes have tripled in size that he felt it too.

Chalk it up to static electricity, because there's no way it would be anything else.

Could it be anything else?

He pulls his hand back, first jabbing it through his hair as if nervously fidgeting and then dropping it to his side. My lips finally unfreeze. "It's not your job to clothe my kid."

"No, it's not." His voice is calm. "But she ruined her shirt on my watch. Plus, I upgraded her wardrobe. I got them matching hockey T-shirts, because she's now one of my biggest fans."

"Aw." My lips slide into a knowing angle. "I get it. You're trying to brainwash my daughter."

"There's no brainwashing. It's a perfectly legitimate clothing option that also happens to level-up her coolness points." There's a playful twinkle in his eyes that's oddly alluring. I try to avoid direct eye contact as he goes on, "Now she has something to wear to the games when you guys come cheer for me."

"I love my new hockey shirt." Bella beams at me. "Jackson said I can wear it to his game tomorrow." It isn't lost on me that Bella's smile is the widest I've seen in a long time. It might be skipping school, or maybe the excess candy, but whatever it is, it fills my heart. Today has been stressful enough, I'm just relieved she's not stressed anymore.

I return my gaze to Jackson as a warm feeling seeps into my gut. On any other day, I would never trust my kid with a near stranger, but it worked out well. Oddly, he did a nice job with the kids. "Uh, we've never been to a hockey game."

"You should try it sometime. One of our biggest games of the year is tomorrow night. Game starts at seven." He meets my eyes with a new look. The worry line that sat above his brow all morning has faded. I like this expression. It makes me believe he's genuinely serious about the invitation.

"We'll see." I shift my weight from one leg to the other and check the time on my phone. "I suppose we'd better get moving. I want to look at the purses, and then we must get to the funeral by three."

"I'm so sorry to hear about the funeral." His playful smile disintegrates into a serious line. "Was it someone close to you?"

"No, I actually don't know them at all." I lift one shoulder into a confused shrug, because I always feel weird confessing this next part. "I'm a funeral singer."

"A funeral singer?" His eyes double blink. "I've heard of wedding singers but never a funeral singer. Isn't that depressing?"

"Not really. I feel useful. I used to sing at weddings, but those are always on weekends. I either have Bella on the weekend and refuse to miss my time with her, or I'm scheduled at my waitress job. Funerals are an odd side hustle, but they're insanely flexible, and bring in extra cash. I can book when it works for me during the week. Usually Bella's in school, so I can attend the service for an hour and there is no extra time commitment." My gaze turns to the kids near the candy machines. They are turning the knobs to see if more candy comes out. Sure, it's sort of like stealing, but what adult doesn't have that childhood memory? "I'm not sure how it's going to go with two kids with mustaches in tow, but I owe you one."

"No, problem. I owe you. I could never bring Rigsby to my press conference. Speaking of which, I need to run or I'm going to be late." Jackson pivots, waves goodbye to Rigsby, and moves toward the door while calling back, "I'll text you as soon as I'm done."

"Thanks again for the mustaches." I smirk at him until he turns the corner then I step between the kids to reestablish control. "Alright kids. I hear you got into a mess at the art place. Consider that your one chance for the day. We are going to a funeral and it's in a church. I need you to be on your very best behavior. No running, no talking—just sit in the very back of the room until I get you."

The dual set of innocent eyes flashing perfect gazes at me doesn't fool me for a second. It's a little bit horrifying as I consider all the ways they can get into trouble, but I don't have another option.

I point to the back aisle. "Before we go, I need a new purse. Just something cheap that has a working zipper."

The kids stumble forward, like they forgot how to work their feet, and I walk slowly in front of them so they don't get lost. In the middle of the center aisle is a table with clearance perfume boxes. A soft peach box catches my eye, and since the kids are moving insanely slow, I pause in front of it to wait.

Chloe.

I'd know that box anywhere.

My mother was once gifted with the bath talc. She wasn't one of those moms who spent much time getting ready, but she used that powder. I loved walking into the bathroom after she'd shower while the musky scent lingered. It was only natural that when I was old enough to wear perfume, Chloe was one of the first ones I "borrowed" from her. I actually remember putting it on for my very first date. A shy kid from my English class who took me to a school dance. I'd never felt prettier than when I put on my mother's signature scent.

I think it worked too, because when I opened the door to meet my date, his eyes sprang wide. Instead of saying hi, his jaw dropped and he said, "Wow."

It's funny how memories remain vivid. For some reason, this one is especially clear today, causing a reminiscent smile to tug at the corners of my lips. I pick up the lovely sample bottle, spritz it into the air, step into it and inhale the floral notes, hoping to relive that moment of feeling beautiful.

Something else rings in my ear.

You smell like stress and dirty dishes.

I instantly put the bottle down, my fingers actually tremble as I align the bottle back into a perfect row with the other samples.

"What are you doing, Mom?" Bella's eyes lock on my shaking hand.

I lift my hand to scratch my ear and turn my back to the table. Hanging my head a little low and feeling silly, I say, "I was just remembering someone I used to know."

"Who was she?" Bella's brows furrow into a contemplative position as she stops behind me. I walk to the single rack of purses. There isn't much to choose from, just two color choices—tan or black. I don't need to check the price. I can tell from the plastic hardware and unbendable fake leather that they don't cost much. I double-check the zipper, and glance at Bella. Instead of answering her question, my lips part.

It's a rarity that I think she looks like me, but from this angle, her eyes shine with so much interest, I'm flooded with a flashback to the days when I was filled with curiosity and zest for life. I used to marvel at things with awe. Now I'm in just a state of survival, I don't even try on a purse before I grab it. Everything is always a rush.

Maybe I'm still stressed from this morning? I'm not usually this emotional but getting a rare bird's-eye-view of my life, I'll be honest, I hate the clarity.

How did I get to this point of life where I'm merely existing in survival mode? An overwhelming sadness floods my heart. I could tell Bella that *She* was nobody special, because I don't want to talk about it. She'll drop it, but that only makes this sting so much worse.

And it's not true.

I raise my chin higher. "I was remembering how I used to be when I was younger."

"How was that?"

"Not like this." My words were soft but factual. "I had a lot of friends. I was hopeful, pretty, and apparently I smelled better." I sigh, because it isn't just about my smell. I used to be pretty too. I used to turn heads. Men used to ask me out. Not that I want to go out with anyone, but it's that feeling that I miss. The feeling of being desired.

Rigsby pipes up. "My uncle said you were pretty."

"Excuse me?" I bark a laugh trying to cover up my instant blush. "W-what did he..." I stutter to a pause and try again. "He spoke about me, hmm? When was this?" I bumble, feeling as if I just pounded fourteen shots of espresso. My heart slams against my rib cage, warning me to put up my guard. My breath is faint, almost transparent as I manage to say, "Your uncle said I'm pretty?"

"He said you were gorgeous but annoying."

"He said gorgeous." The word sticks in my throat, plugging my airway. My defenses weaken like a wall of bricks ready to crumble at the first disappointment.

Gorgeous is good, right?

Not like dirty dishes.

A kink springs in my neck, and I struggle to clear my airway. It draws my ear near my shoulder, but I can't resist thinking about him—his name, that perfect manly name that slips off my tongue so easily, his voice, and that crooked smile.

There.

I finally admitted it. It's not like I'm blind and hadn't noticed how adorable he was, but I was clearly avoiding thinking about it. Because why would I think about it—ahem—him.

I'm a single mom who smells like dirty dishes. I wouldn't think about him, because he wouldn't think about me.

Except, Rigsby said he did.

"When did h-he . . . when did he say that?" I struggle to keep my tone cool, hiding my sudden anxiety.

"Can I help you with anything?" A store clerk peeks her head into the aisle, inserting herself into the conversation.

She takes me by surprise, and I startle, holding up the purse. "No, I found what I need. I'm ready to pay."

Swiping her hand in a smooth gesture, she points to the front. "The cashier can help you."

"Thank you." I smile at her, then my gaze goes back to Rigsby, who is studying his handful of candy. I decide not to ask my question again. That would be awkward.

Even though I'm dying to know more.

"Oh, Mom," Bella grabs my hand and pulls me forward like she has marching orders. "Let's go already."

"Alright," I whisper, holding the bathroom door wide open and using my free hand to silently gesture for the kids to walk forward. I took one last stab at getting the mustaches off. Was I successful-meh? There's still a faint line above each of their lips. On any other day, it would be funny, but it doesn't exactly scream showing proper decorum and respect. I don't know this family. I hope they aren't offended that I brought the kids. I'm doing my best to slip in, sing what I need to sing, and disappear as soon as I can.

Setting an example, I walk at an exaggeratedly slow pace. With one finger to my lips to visually remind the kids not to talk, I glide through the church and find a couple of empty seats in the last row. I wave them forward and keep a stern eye on them while they sit.

Bella's still toting around Little B, and she rests the bear on her lap. At first, I said no to Little B coming inside. Then I figured the bear might help keep her quiet. Also, it could bring comfort since she's never been to a funeral, and I have no idea how she'll react. Rigsby seems content as he leans back in the pew and crosses his arms over his chest. His cheek hollows, as he's still sucking on candy. In another situation, I might ask him to spit it out, but if it keeps him sitting silently for the next hour, I'll allow it. Especially since I can't sit next to them.

I take one more moment to put my finger to my lips and whisper, "Shush." Then I straighten, steel my shoulders, and stride to the piano to take my seat. People bustle in, filling almost every pew in the church. If I crane my neck, I can see the family lined up with the casket in the back. That's my cue to start. I take a deep breath and play the first chord on the piano, keeping one eye on the kids and the other on my music.

God must have blessed this family, because everything goes smoothly. I let out a giant sigh of relief when the last piano chord is struck. The church has mostly emptied. I have a clear line of sight to the kids. They are exactly where I told them to be.

Never have I wanted to shout hallelujah more.

One of the family members walks up to me with an envelope and hands it to me. "Thank you so much. It was beautiful."

"You're welcome." I take the envelope, adding an empathetic expression.

"I'm hoping it's not a burden, but I want to ask if you could follow us to the gravesite. I know my father will smile down from heaven if we sing "Amazing Grace" as the final goodbye."

"Uh." My eyes dart to the kids—still perfect. It's not unusual for people to request gravesite songs, but it's also common enough that I anticipated it. I was totally hoping to be done.

I look back at her. How can I say no to this last request?

"Sure, I'd love to." I hope my smile is believable as I nod and listen to her express her appreciation. I don't hear a word she says, my heart slams warning shots in my chest. The kids were perfect angels in church. I lucked out, but can I really luck out twice in one day? I'm about to find out.

"This isn't so bad," I whisper under my breath, holding a child's palm in each of my hands. The sky is overcast and chilly, with the breeze adding to the discomfort. Risby has another candy tucked in his cheek. Since it muffled him at the church, I'm going with it again. Bella's content with Little B wrapped in her arm. I'm able to stand by the kids during the prayer, and they are perfect.

This is easy.

I have no idea why Jackson had so much trouble at the art museum. These two are like little mice. Before I know it, it's time for the final song, and I lead the group in a cappella as they take turns tossing a rose from the wreath into the grave. It truly is the most touching goodbye I've ever been a part of. The kids stare with wide eyes, not moving so much as a toe until the last person drops their flower.

Feeling it's my duty to be respectful, I hang back, letting the family walk away at their own pace. I turn to the kids and heave a huge sigh of relief. "You guys were amazing. Thank you so much. We can go now." I motion them to go ahead, and they start walking ahead of me. So relieved everything went well—as it was beautiful—I happily offer a treat. "Time for ice cream."

"Ice cream in the middle of the day?" Bella looks back while she continues to stride, her brows shooting high. "Before dinner?" Just then, a root catches her foot, tripping her. She flops forward, and Little B shoots from her arms—*right into the open gravesite!*

"My bear!" Her cries are immediate, and if I'm being honest, *so are my tears.* That bear has been with us since the day she was born. I rush to the edge of the hole and stare down. Little B landed among the flowers, at least six feet down. I'm not going to risk reaching in, because with my luck I'd fall in and get stuck down there. "Mama," Bella sniffs, "can you reach it?"

"I can't." My breath is shallow. It's one of those times when I feel completely helpless. I scan the graveyard for the grave digger, hoping he might have something that can reach down there, but the place is empty. A strange calm washes over me as I stare at Little B resting by the flowers. I turn to Bella, wrapping my arm around her shoulder. "I'll see if I can call someone who takes care of the graves. I'm sure someone can grab it for you."

Bella's eyes are wide as she stares into the hole, tears brimming in her eyelids, and I'm fighting tears too. "Okay." Her confidence is forced as she turns to me, and we trudge back to the car. The shock of losing Little B keeps us all silent, and I suddenly wish I'd been the one responsible for the mustaches.

There is a lifetime of memories in that bear.

Losing Little B is so much worse.

Ten

JACKSON

I round the corner of the ice cream parlor on Main Street and exhale a pent-up breath. The press conference was grueling. It seemed that every sports reporter had picked up on the rivalry between Granite Ice and Noah's new team. I hate that they are making our former teammate into an enemy. Thankfully, most of the questions weren't for me, but I'm still glad it's over. Now I need to grab Rigsby, and I can finally be done with this day. As much as I love spending time with my nephew—and I'm glad I helped my sister—I'm not going to lie and say this day hasn't been stressful.

"Uncle Jack!" I'd know Rigsby's voice anywhere. I turn and find them sitting at a long table by the front window. All three have ice cream sundaes the size of salad bowls in front of them, every color topping mashed like an abstract mosaic.

There's an empty seat next to Rigsby, and I slide in, first making eye contact with Rigsby, then quickly leveling my gaze with Kaci. It's random, and completely unexpected but my heart skips a beat.

I fight the urge to suck back a deep breath, and manage a casual, "How did it go?"

"Funerals are boring," Rigsby's tone is like a foghorn, stressing the first syllable on boring. He doesn't elaborate, shoveling another spoonful of ice cream into his mouth.

"I would assume it wasn't entertaining as that's not the point." I notice chocolate syrup smeared on Rigsby's cheek. Grabbing a napkin from the pile in front of me, I proceed to wipe it. Apparently, I'm turning into my mother.

"It went mostly okay," Kaci says while slightly tilting her head toward Bella—who now that I look at her, has a vacant expression on while her eyes glue to her ice cream. It's not the typical excited way a child should look at ice cream. Her slack jaw and slumped posture are the most telling signs of this conversation.

"What happened?" I direct my question at Kaci with a softened voice.

"Everything was fine." She drops her hand around Bella's shoulder and gives her a squeeze. "They were amazingly well-behaved. I had to go to the cemetery, where Bella tripped, and her favorite bear flew right into the open grave." She arches her hand to illustrate how it flew and adds, "Nobody was around to help me. I wasn't going to crawl down there. I'm going to see if I can get ahold of someone who manages the cemetery before they close it up, but there wasn't anyone at the city office to answer my calls today. I'll try again in the morning."

I visualize the bear flying into the grave. On any other day it might be funny. However, to a child who lost her favorite toy, I understand why she's devastated. "That's awful. I'm sorry that happened."

Bella dips her head lower over her ice cream, which is starting to resemble something closer to soup. As if this horrible day needs a metaphorical cherry on top, Rigsby's elbow slips off the table, and his hand jerks to the left, swooshing his sundae to slide toward me.

I'm about to wear it.

I'm lightning-fast and stop it with both hands, preventing it from tipping off the table, but not from spilling over the side of the bowl.

"Whoa." I slowly slide the bowl back to safety. "Be careful, buddy."

"Sorry." His lips pull down in an apologetic wince.

"Nice save." Kaci hands some paper napkins to me. Our fingers brush together for a mere moment, but the skin-on-skin contact sends an electric zap to my heart. I do a double take back at her. I've never had this reaction to anyone, and it's so odd. My skin warms just being next to her, as if it's attuned to her presence.

Fumbling with my napkin, I succeed in wadding it into a giant sticky ball. My hands are sticky, and this paper napkin only makes it worse. I stand, peeling the napkin off my fingers, and excuse myself. "I'll be right back. I'm going to go wash my hands."

I toss the napkin into the trash on the way to the bathroom, and the young woman working behind the counter catches my attention and asks. "Can I get you an ice cream?"

"Nah." I shake my head, doing my best not to touch anything. I don't want to get anything sticky. "I'm only here to meet those guys but thank you."

"Ah, yes." Her gaze shifts back to Kaci and the kids sitting up front. "You have such a beautiful wife and kids. You're a very lucky man."

"She's, uh, not..." I pause, choking up and trying again, "That's not my...uh." I curl my fingers into a fist and pound on my chest, trying to break the pressure, but it's strange how I can't speak.

Where did this sudden burst of emotion come from?

There's no reason to explain to this woman that Kaci isn't my wife. She doesn't know either of us, and it doesn't matter—but I should at least be able to get the words out.

"Oh, here." She reaches under the counter and grabs a few packets of wet napkins and slides them across the counter to me. "Take these for your kids."

"Thank you." I manage to smile while the words "they aren't my kids" cling to the tip of my tongue.

Those words are broken.

And I don't know why.

Or maybe I do know why.

Maybe it's because deep down, I sort of wish they were my kids. I've always seen myself as a family guy. Although, I've never put a timeline on that sort of thing as I always assumed it would fall into place when it was meant to happen. After today and spending a whole day in the chaos of parenthood, I've been given a taste of what that life could be, and my heart feels a little bit hollow. I've been shown what I'm missing out on. Sure, it's a lot more stress, but it's also a lot more fun. Not to mention, I wasn't bored or lonely once today as I didn't have time for either of those emotions.

I'm stuck with all my words clogging my throat while she returns to her work. Maybe I don't need to explain to her, but something is happening inside my chest that I need to figure out for myself. I retrieve the wet napkins and force my legs to walk back to the table.

My vision morphs into a weird haze, hyper-focused on Kaci, and a single word rings round my head.

Wife.

That's so crazy that the lady thought Kaci was my wife and these are my kids. I'm just babysitting. A forced chuckle leaks out of my brain. Kaci turns to me, meeting my gaze, and a tsunami crashes over, blanketing all my thoughts, leaving only her image embedded in them.

What is happening?

I take one of the wet napkins and clean off the ice cream while my ears ring with the word wife sounding louder and louder in my head.

I'm losing it.

I'm about to smack the side of my head to try to reset my hearing because this is totally crazy, but I don't want to look insane.

"Great idea." Kaci cuts off my ear ringing, extending her hand for one of the wet napkins.

I hand her one, open the remaining packet, and hand it to Rigsby, directing him to clean his hands, while my heart beats like a bass drum, warning me.

Warning me about what?

I have this alarm going off in my chest, but I don't know why.

My heart thrums against my chest, as if announcing, "That's your wife—you're wasting your shot."

I mentally argue back.

What shot?

Since I apparently now have this weird split personality thing going on, my brain responds with a rebuttal that makes my blood run cold.

"How did you miss this before? It's a ready-made family. If she leaves now, this day will be one of those random memories we both tuck away about the worst day ever."

Okay, so what? I argue back.

On cue, my brain rattles back, "What if you were brought together for another purpose? A purpose that's slowly slipping away."

What is going on?

I barely know this woman, and you are trying to tell me she could be my wife? This is absurd.

Sweat pours from my palms as panic seeds in my chest. I feel like I need to stall—to say something, anything—to give me a few more minutes until I can figure out what's going on. "Uh, do you guys have any plans for this evening?" I ask casually, using the last clean spot on the wet napkin to wipe the edge of the table in front of Rigsby.

"Not really." The sigh she emits is mixed with relief and exhaustion. "Just the usual. Dinner and homework for me. I assume the kids don't have homework because of the field trip. So, maybe watch some TV. What about you? Do you have practice?"

"Uh, no. We only practice once a day. I'm usually in bed early, but Rigsby's dad's going to grab him later, so he can meet the new baby. We have some time though. If you're up for one more stop, I have an idea that Bella will love."

"You want to go somewhere else?" Her hand slides over her hair, smoothing it down. Oh, man, she's a gift to humanity. How did I not notice that before? Maybe because she's no longer scowling. She suddenly has this new way of looking at me with a soulful expression, complete with a pouty lip. "Is it far?" she asks.

"Not far at all." I hang onto her gaze, as if challenging her to look more deeply into my eyes. A switch has flipped in my brain. It's my mission to convince this woman that we're perfect together. I'm not exactly sure how that's going to happen, especially when we spent most of the day fighting—but whatever I do, it needs to happen soon. I will not be a fallen soldier in the friend zone, or worse yet, just a forgotten acquaintance.

Back that up. Friend zone is much worse. That's where you hang out and must listen to all the jerks she is dating.

Nope. That will not happen.

I snap my gaze at the kids. We don't even ask them if they want to go. Rigsby is already sliding off his chair, and Bella's eyes lock on me with curiosity as she pipes up, "What is it?"

"It's something you're going to enjoy the most." I extend my hand out, gesturing for her to go ahead, and we all meander to the door. "Okay, kids," I call a little louder, so they follow my directions. "Zip up your coats. We're taking a left, and then we walk two blocks."

The kids bolt ahead, leaving Kaci and me to hang back. For the first time all day, we are alone. Sort of. "So," I let out a long sigh. "The woman in there thought you were my wife."

It's a test.

I want to see what her reaction is to those words. I give her a side-eye and my best flirty smile while the top of her ears turn pink.

Not red hot like she's mad.

More like she's blushing.

Could she be attracted to me as I am to her?

And she's blinking.

Like a lot.

I lose count of how many times. Too much blinking. Blinking feels bad. Until her lips slightly part, and I fix my gaze on the corners of her perfectly formed lips, waiting for a giggle or some hint of how she feels, but nothing comes out.

I smile bigger. My ego inflates a smidge since she didn't outright laugh at the idea. Our steps fall into sync, and I stuff my hands in my jacket pockets as a cool breeze sweeps around us, carrying her scent to me. Fresh floral essence, like a winter haven.

I've never been shy, and since I feel like we're on some sort of time limit, I don't hesitate to tell her, "Has anyone ever told you that you smell amazing?"

Her lips part as she releases a sharp hiss followed by a shallow chuckle. "Not recently."

The kids stop at the corner, and I raise my voice, projecting it forward. "Stop and wait for us before you cross." Then I laugh light-heartedly, peering at Kaci. "This parenting thing is not for the weak."

"You can say that again." Her eyes stay locked on Bella up ahead. We finally catch up with the kids, and I point to the toy store on the corner. "Right in here, kids."

"Build-A-Bear." Kaci's expression twists with questions, and she whispers under her breath, "I don't think we should go in. These bears are all like forty dollars, and it's not in my budget, not after having to fix my car today—"

"My treat." I open the door as far as it goes and usher everyone inside. "Bella gets a new bear, and Rigsby, get whatever animal you want."

The kids push past us, both fitting through the doorway at the same time, and they head to explore their options. Kaci hangs back with a hesitant expression. "You don't have to buy her one of these."

"Your daughter just lost her most prized stuffed animal." It's clear she's not convinced because she's not moving forward. I drop my hand on her lower back and give a gentle press, trying to reassure her and coax her along. Not going to lie. A whoosh zips through my gut when I touch her. "Let me do this for her."

She finally joins Bella and Rigsby, and I stand back, taking it all in.

My heart inflates, never feeling this full before. I know these aren't my kids, and Kaci is far from my wife, but I can't help but think this is what random days with a family would feel like, and I'm soaking it all up.

Eleven

KACI

I can feel Jackson's gaze behind us. Maybe that's why my fingers have the urge to tremble. As I guide Bella to the stuffing machine, my heart crawls farther up my throat. She picked out a bear, the same golden blonde as Little B. It's not surprising, and yet it is. You'd think that after having the same bear all these years, she'd want something different.

"Her name is Little B 2, and she's Little B's sister," Bella says as we move down the line. Her eyes sparkle as she watches the bear get stuffed.

"I'm getting a dalmatian," Rigsby replies. "Just like the one I always wanted for real. And because they didn't have a ferret."

"That's a good call." Jackson chuckles as he comes up from behind me, leaning closer to talk near my ear. "And what are you getting?"

"Oh, none for me, thanks." I shift my weight to the opposite leg, leaning away from him. It's not that I mind standing this close to him.

I don't.

I enjoy looking up at him and seeing the tiny lines in the corners of his eyes, but ever since my run-in with Chase last night, I've been overly self-conscious about how I smell, despite what Jackson said outside. It's been a long day, and there's nothing fresh about my makeup. If I smelled like stress yesterday, I can't imagine what I smell like today.

Jackson pulls an appalled face. "You have to get one too."

"A stuffed animal?" A surprised laugh trickles up my throat. "I've long since outgrown those days. Now if you offer me a washer and dryer, then I'd be smitten," I risk a joke and laugh at it.

"What's your favorite animal?" His voice is insistent as he steps forward, surveying them.

My brain is numb. It's been so long since I thought about what I like. "I don't have one."

"We need to fix that," he murmurs and fake cringes like he's in pain. "What about a favorite color?"

"It used to be purple, but honestly, I haven't thought about it for a while."

He waves toward the display of animals. "Come over here and pick something out, or I'll choose for you—and don't be mad if it's a giant warthog."

"They don't have warthogs." I chuckle as it's crazy for him to spend money on a stuffed animal for me. I never expected him to do that for Bella, and it's wasteful to add another one. "It's a very sweet gesture." I'm struggling to make eye contact. I get it—he's used to women fawning over him, and this is just how he flirts. But I'm not in my flirting era. "What you're doing for Bella is more than enough." When I hesitate to go with him to pick something out, he snatches my hand and pulls me forward.

"Stop being so stubborn. Get in line and pick one out." His words accompany a lighthearted chuckle, telling me he's happy to do this. I don't know why it is so hard for me to accept one kind gesture. Maybe it's another one of those things that has been so long since it happened, I've forgotten how. Or maybe it's because when Chase would find a rare occasion to do something nice for me, he'd later hold it against me. I just don't ever want to be vulnerable like that again.

Plus, he's still holding my hand, and it's sending waves of heat up my arm.

All it takes is for his thumb to brush against my palm, and my shield against him starts crumbling. What is going on? I look at him, and he stares at me as if he's challenging me to drop his hand. All other senses completely shut off, I'm only aware of the sensation of having his skin against mine.

A bubble of nerves swells in my gut. It's light and airy, making me want to giggle—man, I haven't felt this in years, if ever. Whatever this sensation is, it seems to block my memories. I can't remember any interaction before this one. I'm not sure that anything is real beyond the heat radiating from his hand. I could so easily close my eyes and melt into these tingles, but—but—but my brain slams to a wall, instructing me to step aside.

I drop his hand.

Nothing dramatic.

Just making it known that we aren't going to be holding hands like two teens. I step aside. There's no point in messing around and flirting with each other.

His eyes flick to the wall of animals. Without asking me a second time, he looks at the guy working and says, "She'll have a butterfly."

My words asking why cling to the edge of my tongue. My heart rapidly pounds against my rib cage. He's playing a game. I don't need to get sucked into it. I never dated much, but the few guys I did date only wanted to use me. It took me a long time to see that clearly. I'm not going back to that—even if my hand is still tingling.

It isn't like me to be smitten because of a guy paying attention to me.

I don't fall easily.

I don't fall at all.

I'm practical and spend all my time doing mom things.

I don't get giddy over a guy buying me a stuffed animal.

Jackson is oblivious to the invisible boundary I'm trying to draw. He leans down, almost brushing his lips against my ear, and says so softly at a candle-blowing out level—"A butterfly because that's what you give me."

My eyes slam shut, and I scream in my head, trying to silence his words but I heard them all.

Somebody put this guy in a penalty box.

The last thing I need is for some dude to play me. Even though I pride myself on putting up a thick shield, I'm quite fragile underneath. Flirting, even a little, isn't helping my shield. I once again step aside, asserting my position away from him.

We move along the line, and I focus on Bella until we get to the heart station. I've never seen this before, but apparently you pick a heart to place inside the stuffed animal. Jackson's eyebrows pitch in anticipation as he looks from Rigsby to Bella, and says, "You have to make a wish on your heart. It's part of the ceremony."

The kids both go right up, and whisper into their little plastic hearts before stuffing them into their animals. My heart aches as I watch Bella so easily excited about this. She's glowing, and I know she'll talk about this part for a long time. I start to follow them to the final station, but Jackson stops me, "Kaci, you forgot your heart." When I risk a look in his direction, I see he's taken it upon himself to grab a heart, and he's holding it out to me. "You have to make a wish before it goes in the butterfly."

"What are my options?" I wince. I meant it sarcastically—to hint that I don't have much luck—but I didn't intend to ask for his advice. Maybe he'll drop it?

Not my luck.

"Go big." He swallows, marking another thought before he adds, "What is your biggest dream?"

"Um, just to finally graduate from college and get a teaching job. Have a normal schedule for Bella."

"Bigger," he whispers, his gaze spiraling at me.

A laugh cracks out of me. "It's taken me eight years to get through college. What is bigger than that?"

"That's logistical stuff about life. Look at this just once." He extends his hand, trying to get me to take that stupid plastic heart. I glare at it. This must be some sort of line or setup. He asks, "What does your heart want?"

This is so completely insane.

He's holding my little plastic heart in his hands, but it might as well be mine—the way it feels it's chipping away at a wall around my own. The way he's looking at me, with his gaze so intensely focused on me like he might actually care what I have to say, a shiver runs right through me.

"To be happy," I say, raising then lowering my shoulder. There is no way I'm going to even think about anything else—let alone tell him, a stranger just ten hours ago, what my heart desires in any detail.

Even if I knew myself.

He holds up the heart, pressing it almost against the tip of my nose. "Once it's sealed in the butterfly, it can never change."

Another chuckle bubbles to the surface, this one nervous. I've never had someone talk to me like this. His eyes are even smiling, yet appear serious as if warning me not to take this silly tradition lightly. "I mean, obviously there are things I want, but I'm not going to say them out loud."

"If you can't be honest with me, at least be honest with your heart." He pushes the heart toward me. I open my palm just in time to receive it, and his fingers brush against my skin. He pulls away, but all I can think about is how I want to touch him again.

What is wrong with me?

Get it together. Kaci.

What would I wish for anyway?

To be his wife. Ope! Where did that come from?

That was clearly left over from his comment earlier.

It doesn't mean anything.

It can't mean anything.

I shudder, then realize it's not really a shudder—more like a glowy, warm feeling, and the tingles return. I'm smiling like I've been given laughing gas.

Stop it, Kaci.

It's a stupid plastic heart for a silly stuffed animal, and this guy is just a player who wants some attention.

He'd take attention from anyone. I just happen to be the girl standing in front of him.

That's it.

Part of me wants to believe I can impart a wish on this plastic heart, and somehow it will set plans in motion. That's all silly. I take the heart and push it into the butterfly, pulling my gaze from Jackson's.

Maybe this works on all the fangirls he hangs out with, but I live in the real world. I'm not going to swoon over this.

When our stuffed animals get the final stitch, Bella lifts her new bear to her chest. squeezing it so tightly, I wonder if we should have doubled the stuffing. Her eyelids flutter shut as she presses her lips to the top of the bear's head, kissing it over and over. It's surreal to see her show any affection to an animal that isn't Little B. I never thought this day would come. Considering the circumstance, I'm overcome with gratitude. At least she's not heartbroken anymore.

So, maybe Jackson's idea worked?

Not as well as he wanted. It clearly didn't fully sway me into thinking he is Mr. Wonderful, but Bella is in love with her new bear. For that I'm relieved. And grateful as my mama heart is full.

"Alright, Bella, baby." I reach my hand out, waiting for her to take it. "I'm glad you got a new bear, but it's been a long day, and it's finally time to go home."

I turn and head toward the door when Rigsby's voice rings out from behind us. "Do you think we can ride the carousel in the park before we go home?"

"Carousel?" Jackson repeats, his voice laces with confusion. "Since when is there a carousel down there?"

"I don't know but look." Rigsby's finger juts forward, pointing to a decent-sized carousel. I don't remember seeing it before, but a few food vendors set up around it, making it look like a winter carnival.

Bella's eyes widen when she catches a view of the colored lights. "Can we go, Mom?"

Checking my phone for the time, I confirm it's almost dinner time, but this day has been such a mess already. Why try to salvage it now? I shrug, giving up. "Sure. Why not. One ride."

"I got this one." Jackson's already handing cash to Rigsby, and with his other hand, he reaches around me, grabs the door before I get to it, and holds it open until we've all walked through. When I pass in front of him, I get a whiff of his scent. It's strong and masculine and doesn't smell like dirty dishes.

I hate that I'm so hung up on that one thing Chase said to me. I'm not normally bitter like this. It's just insane how someone can say a million things to you, but the one incredible mean thing is the one that sticks.

I stare forward as I walk, refusing to look at Jackson.

I'm not crushing on him.

No way.

I don't crush.

I don't even crack.

All of this is going to be over in the morning, because we'll never be forced to hang out together again.

The kids race toward the carousel as if they've been best friends their whole lives. Even though they're moving at top speed, my brain slows their steps, and I capture them in slow motion.

I never wanted to have another baby—not after struggling so hard to raise Bella, but seeing her have a ready playmate makes my heart twinge.

As if reading my brain, Jackson says, "They get along so well."

"Partners in crime."

He throws back his head and laughs as if I said the funniest thing and not the most obvious. Then he looks at me, and his lips curl. "I might be looking for a partner in crime, myself."

"Stop." The thought comes to me first, and I can't believe I actually say it. By the time I realize what I've done, it's too late to take it back. Now I have to defend it. I glance up at him, blinking a few times as I struggle to explain my outburst. "I uh, I get it. You're handsome. You are probably used to women flirting with you, but I just . . . can't."

I wait for him to smugly smile and tease me about how I said he was handsome. I set myself up again.

That's not what happens.

He reaches out like he wants me to take his hand, and I stare at it.

No, I glare at it.

Did he not hear my speech about how I know he gets all the women? It doesn't work like that. I'm not going to take his hand and skip off toward the carousel.

It's such a preposterous thought that I snort right as his fingers brush against my arm.

His touch unleashes the butterflies, but these are not normal ones. They are warm, igniting something deep in my gut. Part of me is stung by the sensation, but the other half is too curious to see what this guy thinks he's doing.

He can't just touch me.

I'm not his.

My brows lower as I watch his hand move up my arm.

I could slap it away.

Should I slap it away?

Before I can expound on that thought, his hand cups my cheek.

Whoa, now I'm really wondering what he's doing, but I'm frozen in place, unable to ask.

His breath is level with mine, and a magnetic force takes over, pulling me closer. Now I'm kissing a man I just met this morning.

Oops.

As his lips surround mine, pulling me into his warmth I melt into them.

Maybe not oops?

But whatever this is needs to stop before...before...I forget I don't like him.

Twelve

JACKSON

Kaci pulls away, but I dip my chin to her ear. "Kaci." Her name burns in my throat, and it comes out like a command. Everyday pucks fly at my head at a hundred miles an hour, but my heart has never hammered harder in my chest.

I get it.

It was completely assuming.

I should have asked.

She deserved something more romantic than me forcing my lips on hers, but she kept insisting I wasn't genuine in my flirting.

I got her message loud and clear.

She wasn't buying my words. I needed a plan B, and fortunately, I have quick reflexes.

"Uh." Her breath rushes out as she presses her fingertips to her lips, and stares up at me, eyes wide.

I get that it was impulsive.

We just met. That doesn't stop me from plucking her fingers off her lips, taking her hand in mine, and bringing it to my lips, pressing a kiss on her knuckles. "In case you are wondering if that kiss was an accident," I say, "I meant to do that."

She tilts her head closer and harshly whispers, "What is going on?"

"I don't know." I'm not indecisive in my tone. I'm stating a fact.

It's the truth, and I confess the only thing I understand. "I have no idea what is going on, but as the hours ticked down, and I knew you'd be leaving, I just had to do it."

She smirks, not sarcastically, but one I haven't seen before. It's gentle, yet direct. "You just wanted to kiss me," she repeats, her face growing more serious like she's studying math problems. As her brows pin together, she draws a breath, and her tone adds snark, "You just think you can kiss random women whenever you want?"

"No." I haven't lost my sanity. How do I explain that I was running out of time, and she wasn't taking my subtle hints?

There was logic.

Some.

Okay, not logic.

More like something that's the opposite of logic mixed with chemistry.

That's what we have. "I ah, thought we had chemistry, but I didn't know how to say it to get you to accept it."

She has the audacity to roll her eyes, as if I'm not standing right in front of her, watching. "That's a line," she mutters, taking a step closer to the carousel.

I snort laugh and then laugh again. "You think I'm smart enough to have lines?"

She gives me a pointed look, but I don't let her speak. "Tell me that you didn't think that kiss was the best kiss you ever had, and I'll grab Rigsby, and we'll go on our way." I shove my hands in my coat pockets, waiting for her to spit back her rebuttal. Her perfect bottom lip moves, but no sound comes out. It's as if she is dumbfounded.

"Well?" I entice her to speak.

Again, with the eyeroll. Then she says, "I'm not telling you anything unless you feed me."

"Feed you?" I blink and then blink again. That sounds like she's asking me to ask her out without asking me. "Ah, you want to get something to eat?"

"It's dinner time." She nods toward the kids, who are getting off the carousal and heading this way.

"Ah, what do you like?" I gesture as I'm willing to give her anything. At this point if she asked for my wallet, I'd just hand it over without hesitation.

"I'd like to talk about this,"—she gestures between us—" but the kids are going to be hungry." Her gaze shifts past me to the kids, and she speaks as if she's thinking out loud, "How about . . . pizza at my place?"

"Your place?" I deadpan.

"That's what I said." Her light blue eyes move over me as if she's assessing. "It's been a grueling day, and I just want to go home and eat. It's too cold to stand out here and argue about this."

Wow. How brazen.

Maybe that's the theme of the day. We banded together to get through our day and made it this far. Why stop now?

My stomach rumbles. I'm not sure if it's hunger from the mention of pizza, nervous at the thought of talking, or maybe excitement at the possibility of more kissing. Apparently, my stomach gurgle is loud enough that it caught Kaci's attention, and she's staring at my midsection. I'm so insanely thankful I do five hundred sit-ups a day. I leak out a nervous laugh. "I guess my stomach agreed for me."

"Well, what are you waiting for?" She flashes me another new smile. I love this one even more than the last—it's higher on one side, and a tad wobbly. It's smile perfection.

After the day I've had, I'm not one bit surprised I still have Rigsby. I texted Jackie and offered to keep him overnight again. She didn't hesitate to take me up on my offer since she still hasn't delivered the baby. She mentioned they might be having an emergency c-section if it goes much longer, and I told her not to worry. I'll handle Rigsby.

Kaci leads the way inside her apartment building, calling over her shoulder, "I hope it's okay. I already ordered pizza." She flashes her phone at me with a growing-hangry smile on her face. "I have the app."

"That's fine." We stop at the door, and she selects one key from her jumbo-sized key ring, sliding it into the lock until it clicks.

"Never mind the mess. I haven't been home all day, or really much at all lately." She strolls ahead of us into the apartment and shuffles a few stacked Amazon boxes to the side, clearing a path for us to walk. Then she stops at a hook on the wall and hangs up her coat.

Bella kicks off her shoes and hands her coat to her mom. "Can I show Rigsby my room?"

"Just until we eat." Kaci places Bella's coat on the hook next to hers. Then she reaches forward for Rigsby's coat and adds it on top of Bella's. "When the pizza gets here, we are eating at the table. Then it's going to be time to wash up for bed. It's been a long day."

Kaci's eyes follow the kids as they pad down the hall. Then she slowly turns to me, letting a quiet sigh slip from her lips. "Well."

"So." I rock back on my heels. Everything is happening so fast. I'm not quite sure what I'm even doing here. I get that she's hungry, but she certainly didn't need to invite us over.

"Come in. Can I get you something to drink?" She gestures toward the couch that's only a few steps inside. It's a tiny apartment—a TV, couch, and coffee table in the living room, and a small kitchen on the opposite wall. She crosses the room, taking a moment to fix the pillows on the couch as she passes, and continues to the fridge, opening the door. "I, ah, I have juice boxes, water, or I can make some coffee."

I meander to the sofa, plopping down right as her gaze shifts back to mine. "Water is fine."

"Sorry." She grabs two bottles of water, shuts the door with a swing of her hip, and returns to the center of the room, passing a bottle to me. "I wasn't planning on having company or I would have had something else to offer."

"Water's perfect." I must have sat on a spring or something, because there's a hard spot. I shimmy over, placing me more in the center of the couch.

"Good." She slowly lowers herself onto the couch. Since I'm now in the middle, there's only a slice of air between us.

I resist the urge to gulp. I'm not a gulper, so I have no idea where that came from. It's like I have a comment ready to fly out of my mouth, and I'm trying hard to play it cool. The problem is, that she's gazing at me in a new way—a way that makes me want to skip the talking stage and just reach over and steal a kiss.

Again.

She pushed me away last time, so of course, I'm not going to try that again. *Probably not.* But there must be a reason she invited me over.

After twisting the top of her bottle, she says, "We made it through the most insane day. I think we need to toast to our success."

I chuckle, and I tap my bottle with hers. "Cheers to that. I couldn't have done it without you." She tips her bottle and drinks. I take a swig and set my bottle on the small coffee table and turn toward her. "So, nice place. How long have you lived here?"

"Too long." She lets out a huff and places her drink down next to mine. "I've been here since Bella was a baby. I'm ready to move into something with more space as soon as I graduate in May. I'm in my last semester of classes, and then I will student teach next semester, and I'm done."

"Bella's seven." I conclude since I know Rigsby's age. "It's just been you two all these years?"

Her face crinkles as if she's holding back, and her only reply is, "Yep."

"So, Bella's dad..." I drop the question right after it's out and quickly change the topic, "This is a great location."

"It's a fair question." Her gaze deepens, and she pulls a leg underneath her as she leans back into the cushions. My mind enters a time warp—one where we are so comfortable sitting next to each other that I can casually reach over, grab her legs to rest on my lap, and lounge with her while we binge Netflix. I blink away the vision as she continues, "Chase and I co-parent but we've been broken up for years. He gets to see her every other weekend, but it's always just been us."

"Gotcha."

"So, how are you enjoying being a parent?" A teasing gleam sparkles in the corner of her eye, and it does everything to put me at ease. I sink further into the couch.

"It's been insanity. Clearly, I failed." A loose chuckle slips from my throat, and I shake my head. "If it hadn't been for you helping so I could work, I surely would have gotten fired. I don't know how you do it."

"You learn as you go." Her beautiful eyes, a kaleidoscope of the clearest seas, glitter back at me. "I suppose you got scared off from having any of your own someday."

My lips pull down as I don't know how to answer her. Before today, it felt like it was always a far off someday, but I can't tell her I've been imagining having a family with her randomly throughout the day. "I, ah, enjoy being the fun uncle. Someday I'd like a family. I'm mostly just focused on my career right now. The team's off to a good start this year, and it's a good time. If you want to come to a game sometime, let me know. I can get tickets for you and Bella."

"Maybe."

"Maybe what?"

Her fingers wrap around the back of her neck, and she holds her palm there for a beat, as if she's deep in thought. "I guess maybe it depends why you are asking. Are you asking me out?"

Wow.

That's seriously bold, but I get it. I kissed her. My lips slide into a smirk as I wonder how she can ask me that and keep a straight face.

"I mean." I fill the beat of silence with a shoulder shrug and add a smoldering smile before saying, "Clearly, we have kissing chemistry." I've never been put on the spot like this before, but it doesn't make me want to step back. If anything, her flirting makes me want to banter on. "That was a good first kiss, wasn't it?"

"The execution was good," she replies without missing a beat. "The timing was interesting."

I gesture toward myself, feeling my chest puff out a little. "What do you mean interesting?"

"I wasn't expecting it—that's for sure." She reaches forward and grabs her water again, but instead of drinking, she sets the bottle on her leg and fidgets with the cap.

"Good." I bop my head. "I want to keep you on your toes."

Her gaze drops to her bottle, and her lips cave down. When she finally speaks, her voice is broken. "I appreciated your help today, and ah, thanks for the kiss and all. It's been a long time since I felt...well, wanted like that." She pauses, and her throat bobs, as she swallows deeply.

I resist the urge to reply because the expression on her face is pained. Eventually, she levels her gaze with mine. "Look, I've got a lot going on here. I'm finally getting my life almost on track. I'm finishing my degree. I'll be starting a new career in teaching. And Bella." She glances at the door adjacent to the living room, and her voice fades with the last part: "I'm so insanely flattered, but I just don't have room for a distraction."

"Whoa." My defenses rise along with my eyebrows. "You sure get right to the point, don't you?"

She adds an unapologetic shrug. "I have a lot to consider...and I'm done screwing up my life. I've done enough of that."

"What do you mean screwing up?" I gesture around me. "It looks like you're doing pretty good to me. You have a cute place and a great kid."

"I have an amazing kid, but you know what I'm talking about." Her eyes snap back at me, challenging me. "I mean...I'm done loving people who are wrong for me. I'm not going to be somebody's fling, so yeah, thanks for the kiss." She slopes her chin up, as if physically placing a punctuation mark to end the conversation. "I'm not going to play around and pretend this could lead somewhere. You're having fun playing funcle, but I do this full time. Our lives are clearly different."

The way she cuts to the chase, not leaving any room for misunderstanding, makes the tension thick between us. "I sort of feel like you're making a lot of assumptions about me. Who said anything about a fling?" I quirk an eyebrow in offense. "Did it ever occur to you that I might be interested in more than that?"

"Let me guess. You say that to all the girls." She gives me a pointed glare.

"No." I wait, like I've lost my mind, because this woman—who I've known for less than twenty-four hours—has me acting completely out of character. The way she's challenging me, pushing me away before I even have a chance to find out if I want to get close to her, has me fighting back.

She dips her chin again and rubs her eye. Maybe she's tired but a part of me wonders if she's getting emotional and pretending her eye bothers her to hide something...maybe tears? "I don't know how else to explain this to you," she continues, "but I've made so many mistakes, and I'm so far behind in life. For Bella's sake, I can't afford to risk anymore."

Mistake?

"You don't even know what this could be. How can you say I'm going to be a mistake?" The way she looks at me says it all.

This isn't about me or her not feeling this chemistry. This is about her inability to move forward. I stare at her, but she refuses to meet my gaze.

She's clearly not wanting anything more from me. I'm not going to push myself on her—or anyone—but at this point, my anger rises. Not because she doesn't want to get to know me more, but because she's shut herself off completely. She can reject me, but she's an incredible woman who deserves to believe she's worthy of love.

I purse my lips, mulling over all the things I could say. "You know." I reach out, unable to stop myself from touching her arm. She stiffens the moment my fingers brush her skin. I hold my hand steady, making sure she doesn't turn away because I need her to hear what I have to say. "You're focusing on your past mistakes. If you went back to erase all your mistakes, you'd delete yourself.

That would be a shame because you seem like an amazing woman to me."

Her eyes brim with tears, she jumps to her feet and turns her back toward me. Taking that as my cue, I stand and call toward the bedroom door, "Rigsby, it's time to go."

"Don't you want to stay for pizza?" Kaci turns her head as she tries her best to discreetly dab at her eyes.

"I appreciate the offer, but you've made your point. You don't need a distraction." I step toward the door just as Rigsby comes out of the room, and I grab his coat off the hook. My tone isn't the least bit harsh. If anything, I do everything I can to show empathy. "Thanks for having us over, and for all the help today. See ya around."

Thirteen

I flip to my other side, forcing my eyes to close, but after only a moment, I give up. It's no use. The sun peeks from underneath my drawn bedroom shades. I might as well use this time to brew an extra cup of coffee because I'm certainly not getting any more sleep. I'm not even tired as I push myself to a sitting position and stretch my hands over my head. It must be some sort of an adrenaline that won't shut off. My mind was active all night.

Of course, I was thinking about Jackson—who wouldn't after that kiss?

Yesterday was insane.

It doesn't even feel real now as I recall it. I mean, what are the odds of everything happening the way they did. It's one thing for me to find his glove, but we both ended up missing that bus. It was incredibly stressful, but the way we banded together to get through our day was actually sort of fun, now that I look back on it. I don't remember the last time I saw Bella laugh as much as she did with

Rigsby. Sighing, I drop my hands to my sides and stand. God was looking out for me by inserting Jackson into my life right when I needed the help for the day. That's all it was.

The corners of my lips tug into a smile as I recall for the gazillionth time *that kiss*.

It did something to me. Like it awakened a sense in me that had been dead for so long. It's uncanny how long it's been since I thought about romance. After Chase bailed, I just shut everything off and never wanted to go there.

Not that I want to go there now.

It was just nice to have a moment like that, where I felt attractive and not like just a mom.

Speaking of being a mom, Bella's footsteps pad down the hall toward the kitchen, and I follow, calling, "Good morning. How did you sleep?"

"Good." She plops into her seat at the table, watching me as I grab her favorite generic cereal bag from the cupboard and milk from the fridge.

"Well, we don't need to worry about missing any buses today, but maybe let's try to leave a few minutes early, just in case I have a problem with my tire." I set her bowl and spoon on the table and then start the coffee pot. I spare her the details since she's only seven. She doesn't need to know the mechanic wanted me to replace the tire—said it was shot—but I just don't have the money right now. Tuition payments are draining every last penny I have. So, he patched it up, and said, "You shouldn't have any problems as long as you don't drive it too much." Maybe it's just my unlucky luck, but something about the way he said that gave me an ominous vibe.

She pours a bowl of cereal as I check the dishwasher for my favorite travel mug. It used to be pink, but most of the enamel coating has worn off. It's not really a favorite as much as it's the best of what I have. My dishwasher is empty, though I don't remember emptying it. Then again, I was up late last night, nervously puttering around in the kitchen. I open the cupboard, find it neatly on the shelf, and retrieve it.

"Do you think we can go to the hockey game tonight?" Bella's words are muffled by the crunching of her cereal, but I hear them perfectly.

I give her a curious look. "Hockey?"

"Yeah, the one Rigsby was talking about. He said they're so much fun, and this game is going to be good because it's against their rival."

I know exactly which game she's talking about, but she's never liked hockey. Not to mention, it will be totally cringe if Jackson sees me there, especially after the awkward conversation last night. I can't believe I almost broke down in tears. The whole thing was terrible. No, there's no way I want to show up there—or anywhere Jackson will be—even if I had extra money for tickets. "Um, I mean, it sounds okay, but it's not really in the budget right now." I hate to discourage her from any interests, but it's an honest answer.

"Okay." Without even a hint of disappointment, her gaze drops back to her bowl, and I marvel at how I got the sweetest little girl on the planet.

My coffee is ready, so I pour my mug and take a sip. It's the perfect sipping temperature to warm and coat my throat. After another sip, I head toward the bathroom but pause to grab my phone off the counter.

I have a text message.

Chase: I'm not going to be able to make it to Bella's school thing Friday. I have band practice. Can you drop her off at my place after?

My heart doesn't fall even a millimeter. I'm numb to his failures, but I know Bella's not. She still looks at him with stars in her eyes. It breaks my heart because he's only capable of making the light in her eyes go dim. My thumb hovers over my phone as I fight the urge to argue with him—for her sake. She deserves better, but I've long since given up on arguing. Now I just think how sad it is that he is missing out on the greatest gift he'll ever know. This message doesn't even need a reply. I delete it.

I turn back to Bella. My mouth opens and closes as I can't decide if I should tell her now, risking ruining her day, maybe even her week, or—keep it to myself, hoping he changes his mind, but risking her being devastated if he doesn't show?

"What's wrong, Mom?" Bella looks at me with a tilt to her head.

"Ah, I got a text from your dad." I hold the phone up, even though the message is gone. "He said to give you a heads-up, that he *might* not be able to make it to your festival this Friday, but he's going to do his best to try."

Why do I lie for him?

Chase doesn't know the meaning of the word try.

I'm not even bitter. It's the truth that settles after someone has had second, third, and twentieth chances. After a while their words become dust on a windy day. However, since yesterday was a disaster, I can't afford to have a repeat day. We need one good day. My eyes lock with hers, and she remains still, as if she's still processing. "Do you think he'll make it?"

I blink. I hate to lie to her. Bella is my biggest blessing, but I regret Chase every day. I'm not going to say yes, because then she'll be upset with me when he doesn't come. I can't say no, because she'll be heartbroken. As much as this life is hard and things happen, we need one good day this week. "I'm hoping he comes."

Instead of cheering up, her face stays neutral, as if she's already letting go of him being there. It tugs at my heart that she has to learn this lesson at such a young age. "You know what?" I blurt out the first thing that comes to mind, just wanting her to have something to look forward to today, so she doesn't waste the whole day being sad about this. "I changed my mind. Let's do the hockey game tonight. It sounds like fun."

Her eyes shift from side to side before a smile slams on her lips. "Are you serious?"

"Yeah." I nod, already mentally preparing for it. If we sit in the nosebleed seats and I wear a coat and hat, there's no way Jackson will even know we are there. The way she looks at me—as if I'm her biggest hero—is worth it. I'm glad I agreed to her suggestion. She'll be in a good mood all day, and it will take her mind off her dad. We deserve this treat for ourselves. "It'll be fun." I nod again, checking the time on my phone. It's almost time to leave, and I haven't even changed out of my pajamas yet. "I'll order some tickets, and we'll plan on it," I say as I turn on my heel and race down the hall.

Fourteen

JACKSON

New plan.

I wear my glove all morning to avoid losing it before the game. It wasn't so much of a plan as it was a new co-dependent anxiety I unlocked. Every time I went to put my glove in my hockey bag, a wave of nausea crashed over me, and I couldn't shake it off. So, instead of walking around with my gut in knots, I just walk around with my glove.

It's fine.

I'm sure it has everything to do with the buzz around tonight's game. I'm not one to get overly nervous about games. I'm used to feeling as if the weight of the entire game rests on my shoulders.

Pressure is my strength.

I love being the calm in everyone else's storm. That's why I've always excelled at being a goalie. As I round the corner to Victory Hall, a flash of light sparks from the arena, and it catches my eyes. I blink but keep walking. More than likely, maintenance is working on the lights.

After a few more steps, I pass another entrance to the arena. A second spasm of light draws my gaze back inside. Now I'm curious. The lights should not be malfunctioning like that. I peek my head inside the door. The arena is mostly empty with the doors not opening to the public until half an hour before the game starts.

Bill Baker is standing by the edge of the rink, holding some remote. He's talking to a couple of guys dressed in dark suits. After talking to one guy, Bill presses a button on the remote, and a giant lightning bolt zaps from a machine above the rink.

Unprepared for how bright it is, I jolt back.

Holy blinding light. I blink, trying to see something—anything. I've gone temporarily blind.

I've seen these lightning machines before, but they aren't *that* bright. I shake my head as it doesn't surprise me one bit that Bill did something to try to outdo Noah's new team. This is a big game for him. I can't imagine how awkward it must be to be rivals with your stepson's hockey team, but he doesn't have to act this way. He can choose to be civil—or at least not blind us all.

It's just not his way of doing things.

I can't stop shaking my head as I continue to the locker room. I'm one of the first guys to arrive, but I'm always the slowest getting geared up. By the time I'm ready, the whole team has arrived. I keep checking the office door behind me, waiting for Bill to come in and have some words to say, but when the door finally opens, it's only Coach Carlson.

"Hey, Coach." I nod as he strolls past me. All the side conversations that were buzzing around the room immediately die. Coach scans the room once. We all hold our breath, waiting for him to say something—the magic words of encouragement that will push us to win—but he's oddly quiet.

"What's up with the lights?" Axl asks, finally breaking the silence, a chuckle slipping from his lips. "I saw Bill got some fancy lightning machine. What does he think, that we're the Voltage now?"

"You guys know how Bill is. Anything for this team, and he wants the fans to be excited for tonight." Coach stuffs his hands into the pockets of his suit coat and leans a shoulder against a locker. It's so rare to see him like this. He's usually more professional, maintaining perfect posture. Maybe his nerves have gotten the best of him?

Wow. I've never heard a pregame speech so anticlimactic that a snort escapes me, drawing Carlson's gaze to level with mine. "Something wrong, Mr. Owen?"

"No." I ball my fingers into a fist and tap on my chest, faking a cough to cover it up. "Something was stuck in my throat."

"That's what I thought." Coach walks in a slow circle, taking time to eye each one of us, and he then steps toward the door, calling back, "Everyone in the tunnel in two minutes."

It's deathly quiet until the door clicks shut behind him, and Axl immediately turns to me. "Wow, you know it's serious when he doesn't even pretend to be excited. He looks terrified."

"You think so?" I grab my helmet, as it's the final thing I need before I'm ready, and stand. I always hold off putting it on until I have to, because goalie gear is in a league of its own when it comes to the sauna effect. Nobody sweats like a goalie in full gear.

"I wonder if Bill threatened his job if we lose?" Axl steps in front of me, and we stride out together, balancing on our skates.

"I don't think he'd do that, would he?" My brows furrow as I stare at Axl.

"Yeah, he would. He traded his own stepson. He'll probably fire us all if we lose." Without waiting for my reply, he slips on his helmet and rushes down the tunnel. I follow suit, not wanting to give coach any reason to be upset with me before the game even starts. Something feels off. The hair on the back of my neck stands up. There's always tension before a game, but this is eerie.

When we skate out of the tunnel, everyone is all business, skating warmup laps. I take my spot in the net and do what I always do when the ice is fresh, skating back and forth to wear down the slick crease.

The crowd is cheering, but it still feels like the vibe is off. I can't resist scanning the arena, starting with the owner's box above my net. Bill's where he always is, which normally doesn't bother me. However, it adds so much pressure with him literally looming over my head, and tonight, it slaps the sweat on my back. The lights flicker on and off, dimming nearly to darkness, and then that weird lightning machine Bill just installed shoots fake lightning from directly above his suite.

The crowd's screams become unhinged, but I'm not convinced this lightning is a good addition.

In another arena I might be okay standing under lightning. I'm not so sure I trust Bill with electricity. After the second bolt of lightning, I find myself glaring at the machine. It's time to do my stretches, and I drop into my splits, staring forward.

Someone yelling my name from the stands catches my attention and I smile. Normally Jackie brings Rigsby, but she's still in the hospital. After a day of laboring, the doctor ended up taking the baby in an emergency c-section. She's fine, and so is the baby—another bouncing baby boy. I smirk, thinking about all the Granite Ice hockey merch this little guy is going to have from his funcle.

Earlier today, I picked Rigsby up from school and dropped him off at the hospital, so he could finally meet his brother. I had wanted to go too, but it's going to have to wait a day. I'm glad I could help Jackie out, but Rigsby was bummed he couldn't make it to the game tonight and wished me super-duper luck with tears brewing. Now, I'm smirking ear to ear.

It looks like Rigsby twisted his dad's arm into bringing him, because they are right behind our goal in the seats I always reserve for him and Jackie. He's always been my number one fan.

Wearing the Granite Ice hoodie I bought him, Rigsby waves a sign that says, "#1 goalie." It's corny, but I always get a surge of warm fuzzies when I see that. It's funny because it's true in more ways than one, especially since that's my jersey number. I love that he's my biggest fan. I'm glad Tom's taking a couple of hours to spend with Rigsby. A new baby is going to be a huge adjustment for him. This little dude's life is forever changed—in the biggest way.

The music switches to the song I always say is my *get-up-a-bro* song, and I stand again. The knot in my stomach is mostly even now. I flick one more glance over my shoulder at Bill, but it's right as the lightning flashes. Such weird timing, and now I'm partially blind again. I squint and wobble on my skates. My gaze falls to the side, but not before something catches my eye. I raise my glove to shield my eyes, still half-squinting from being partially blinded. I can't make out who it is...

I tilt my head to the side.

The girl looks like Bella. I must be seeing things.

I look to the girl's side, and I find myself holding my breath.

Kaci.

Bella and Kaci are sitting way up underneath that stupid lightning machine. Those must be the worst seats in the house. Seeing them catches me off guard, and I turn my back to them. It's time for the faceoff, but for the first time in a long time, my focus is split.

What is Kaci doing here?

I'm not a total idiot. There are only two reasons to be here.

One...to watch the game, which she didn't seem all that interested in, and the other...to see me.

My heart rate ramps up so much, I can feel each beat in my throat. She doesn't like hockey, as she's said herself, which clearly leaves the latter reason to be true.

Now I can't stop smiling, and I'm supposed to have my game face on. I toss another glance over my shoulder: sure enough, she's looking this way.

So much for not needing a distraction. Apparently, she wants to play hard to get.

Good thing for her, I'm amazing when it comes to hard wins.

Fifteen

Kaci

Thankfully nosebleed seats are only seven bucks each. I cleaned the change out of the center console of my car to scrape together enough money for popcorn and drinks. Now, we're sitting way up in the top row, nearly empty except for us—just another reminder that I'm more broke than the average person. It's okay, though. Bella's smile is the largest it's been in a long time, and that makes it worth it.

"There he is, Mom." Bella points forward with urgency like she's spotted her long lost friend. She insisted on wearing the Granite Ice T-shirt Jackson bought her. At first, I hesitated but the only reason I had for her not to wear it had to do with my dwindling pride, and well, she looks adorable in blue and orange.

I scan the ice as the players move into their positions until I land on Jackson. Craning my neck for a better view, I find myself sliding to the edge of my seat. "Yeah, that's him."

With wide shoulders, he commands his space. Maybe it's the arena, or the music, or the fans, but the electric energy in the air instantly pumps me up. Sporting events of any kind are another one of those experiences I haven't allowed myself to enjoy in years. It feels good to be here and to be excited for something. I can't keep my eyes off the team. They are all fast and limber as they warm up. I've never seen a hockey game in real life, and this is beyond what I expected. I expected it to be loud, but this is deafening in the most fun way, as fans stomp their feet in the stands and scream out players' names.

And Jackson takes control. With his goalie pads on, he's everything one would want in a giant man-brick. Not that I know anything about hockey, but that's seriously the only way I can describe him. Not to mention he certainly knows how to wear a jersey. There's so much confidence oozing from him, if I was an opposing player, I would be intimidated.

The guys line up for a faceoff, and the puck is in play with Arctic Force in control. It all goes so fast, and I find my head turning back and forth as I frantically struggle to keep track of the puck. It's only a couple of minutes in, and one of their guys goes to Jackson's net to shoot. I literally hold my breath, suppressing a squeal. I didn't think it would feel like this, but my heart is in my throat.

Jackson's movements are fluid, and he effortlessly blocks the puck, like it's the most natural thing in the world to him. His teammates pound their sticks against the boards to celebrate his impressive save.

Suddenly, I love hockey.

"Mom, did you see that?" Bella asks as she stands up on her seat for a better view. Since there's nobody behind us, I don't tell her to get down.

"I did." I don't even want to talk; it takes away part of my concentration from the game. Granite Ice now has control of the puck, and they are getting closer to the Arctic Force's net. I literally want to put my hand over my heart as it's beating so fast. Granite Ice misses their shot. Artic Force regroups a lot faster, gains control of the puck, and brings it back to Jackson's net again.

I want to close my eyes. I can't even watch this. How does Jackson handle this kind of pressure? The puck literally flies right toward his face, and he gracefully extends his glove and snatches it out of the air. The crowd screams, and the players slam the boards again. I'm so full of energy that I find myself screaming too.

Granite Ice, once again has the puck and takes it back down the ice. I have no idea what any of the player positions are, but the same guy who shot last time attempts another shot. My top teeth crash into my bottom lip. I can't stand the excitement.

Their goalie kicks out a pad, but he misses!

The puck goes in the net, and the crowd's screams become unhinged. I jump and pump my fist in the air. The arena lights dim, and a giant lightning rod rockets above my head. It's so bright, I scream from shock. The arena lights pulse on and then off, leaving us all in the dark. At first, it's a tad funny, but after a moment, fear spreads through the arena and screams echo off the high ceiling.

Darkness remains.

I reach to the side, grabbing Bella's shoulder as the crowd's happy cheers are completely replaced by muffled whispers.

"Mom, what happened to the lights?" Bella asks.

"I don't know." I reach for my phone and turn on the flashlight. "I think that lightning machine must have blown the power or something."

"Everyone, stay seated, please" a voice yells from down below. It's hard to hear because it's not over the speaker system. "We've lost power, but for your safety, we ask that everyone stay seated until we have the lights restored."

"Are you kidding me?" Bella drops to her seat, and slumps down in the chair. "It was getting so good."

"Yeah, that's terrible timing," I mutter as I sit back in my seat, grabbing my popcorn, thankful to have something to do while we waste time. Everyone has taken out their cellphones. There are hundreds of flashlight beams weaving through the air now, and it's crazy hard on my eyes.

"What do we do, Mom?" Bella's wide eyes look back at me.

"Nothing." I shrug. "We just wait." I fold my bottom lip in and check my phone for the time. Hopefully, this delay isn't long—it's a school night. I find myself shaking my head.

What are the odds that the power goes out the one time I actually go to a sporting event?

Sixteen

JACKSON

This is worse than a made-for-TV sitcom!

The game is far from over, but apparently Bill's lightning machine overloaded the breakers or something, and the arena lost power.

We stood on the ice in the dark for a while. At first, it was funny to watch Bill scramble to get someone to look at the machine. There were several electricians in the crowd, but they all seemed to have the same opinion—that parts needed to be replaced. Parts that had to be ordered, which meant the game was over.

We forfeited and took the loss on the biggest game of our season.

Bill can't be mad at us.

This is all on him. I know one thing: I'm not sticking around to hear how upset he is. We use our phones for light, propping them up to help us see the locker room. I'm able to quickly remove my gear, stuffing everything into my bag.

"What's wrong with your face, Owen?" Axl stuffs his skates into his locker.

I was hoping nobody would notice. We just took the most depressing loss of the year, but I can't wipe the sloppy grin off my face. Ever since I saw Kaci, it's stuck there.

Elijah, usually the quiet one, since he's the new guy, leans over and punches my shoulder. "You got facial paralysis from taking too many pucks to the helmet?"

"I think so." They can think that, because I'm not admitting to them the real reason. Kaci's gorgeous face is stuck in my brain. Somehow, she's become my obsession. I don't need to explain any of this to them. They'll just make fun of me.

I'm ready to leave by the time Coach ambles into the locker room. "Nobody leaves, guys." He motions for everyone to sit.

A groan sticks in my throat. Thankfully, I hold it in and lower myself to the bench.

"What was Bill even thinking?" Axl blurts out the question we all want to ask.

"I think we can all agree, he really wasn't." Coach stuffs his hands into his jacket pockets, and a forlorn expression washes over his face. "Apparently, the breakers should have been upgraded, but he was in too big of a hurry to have the machine available for tonight's game, so he instructed the installation team to just force it. So, we will go forward with zero points from this game."

A collective moan ripples through the room. I leak out the groan that's been burning in my throat. Sometimes, it feels like we're owned by a circus ringmaster and not a professional.

"They are vacating the arena now. As for practices," Coach raises his voice above our disgusted muttering, "the arena will be dark for at least a day or two. Tomorrow, practice is at the outside ice rink."

I snort. This doesn't feel real. It's been ages since I played hockey on a frozen pond, and I certainly didn't think I'd be practicing like that once I made it to the AHL.

"Is there any good news?" Axl asks sarcastically.

"That's all I have." Coach shrugs, his head hanging low. I've never seen him so downhearted. Maybe it's the stress of what this game was supposed to be. I let out a heavy sigh, the emotional rollercoaster of the week finally reaching a point of release. Sure, we didn't win, but the game is over. Not the outcome we wanted, but over nonetheless.

And I didn't get fired.

I rise to my feet and shoulder my bag, rotating my wrist in a circle. As I bend my hand back toward my forearm, a sharp pain shoots up my arm. I'm sure it's from that puck I caught. Normally, I'd report it to the team physical therapist, but with the power out, everyone is leaving. I don't care to stick around. I can easily just pop a couple of pain killers, ice it, and get some rest. It should be better in the morning.

I'm a couple of steps out of the locker room, and I'm bombarded by my favorite little person. "Uncle Jack!" Rigsby races out of the dark hallway, and slams into me with a giant hug around my midsection.

I chuckle, not surprised by his resourcefulness and ability to find me in the dark. Tom's profile and phone light appear around the corner. "How'd you get back here with the power off?"

"They were escorting everyone out the main entrance, so we snuck down the back stairs," Rigsby proudly declares.

"Nice, but not really." I motion toward the back exit. "We'd better get out of here before someone catches you. Everyone is in a terrible mood."

"Are you going home?" Tom asks.

"Eventually." I say, bending my wrist again. Another shot of excruciating pain rockets up my arm. It's not getting better. "I might have to stop at the general store for some painkillers. I don't think I have any at my place." I raise my brows in question. "Why? What's up?"

"Oh, can I come?" Rigsby blurts out, his eyes growing wide with excitement.

"To the general store?" I raise my hand and scratch the back of my head, confused about why he'd be excited about that. "Isn't it a school night?"

A laugh rushes out of Tom's mouth. "He's trying to get out of going to the hospital. He likes his new baby brother and all, but he's not a fan of crying. He wanted me to ask if he could go with you instead. He said something about wings and root beer."

My tastebuds instantly awaken at the suggestion. "Ah, sure. It's right next to the general store. We can grab what I need and then eat. I can drop him off at your house when you are ready to go home."

"Are you sure?" Though his words are drenched in a tone of apology, the look he gives me is full of appreciation.

"Not a problem. I'm happy to help out. I'm sure you and Jackie are both exhausted." I summon Rigsby. "Come on, Bud."

He's all smiles as he syncs his steps with mine. I wave to Tom and turn as I'm parked across the lot. "I'll see ya later."

"Thank you," he calls over his shoulders, rushing off in the opposite direction. The breeze has picked up, and it's much colder than it was earlier, causing me to pick up my pace. Rigsby is so comfortable in my car that he climbs right into the backseat without help, and I start the engine and pull out.

"So, how was school today?" I eye him in the rearview mirror. "Did the teacher ask why you missed the field trip?"

"She never said a word about it," his tone infuses with excited inflections. "It was career day, and Aiden's dad came—he's a cop. We got to see his police dog, and that was super fun. And Bella's dad came too—he works in a band, so he gave us all guitar picks."

"Bella's dad was there." It slipped out before I had a chance to think. "What kind of band is he in?"

"It's a real rock band." Rigsby slams his face down into a head bang.

"Um." I resist the urge to pepper him with questions, but it's odd. Kaci made it seem like Bella's dad wasn't overly involved with Bella. While I'm considering all the things that are odd, my mind circles back to how extremely odd it was to see them at the game tonight.

Sure, I invited them, but it didn't seem like they were taking me up on my invitation. Kaci did not give off the impression that she even remotely cared about hockey. Plus, she was sitting at the very top of the arena when there were plenty of seats closer to the ice. She mentioned a few times that money is tight right now. Would she really spend money to go to a hockey game if that's not her thing? Unless there was a reason...

All these thoughts race through my head, and before I know it, I'm parked in front of the general store. Rigsby's already getting out. One thing about him—he reminds me a lot of myself, always a go-getter and asking for exactly what he wants. I already know what he's going to ask for when I pull out my wallet and hand him the few single bills I have. "You can have one candy."

He scurries forward but pauses to open the door for me, which makes me smile. Rather than running directly to the candy, he sticks by my side as I head straight to the first aid section. "What did you say you needed?" He asks, scanning the rows as we pass.

"I need some over-the-counter pain pills or something." I pause in the center aisle where a giant table of clearance items takes up most of the room. I have to literally turn sideways to get around it. It's just piles of unorganized merchandise—lots of summer items, notebooks, crayons, and markers. "Do you need any school supplies?" I motion to the rows of colored glue. I'm half tempted to get some art supplies for my place, especially since Rigsby's been spending more time there lately.

"Nah, my mom gets me all that." He steps to the side so he can get around the table too, but his gaze goes to the end of the adjacent aisle. "Oh, that's the perfume Bella's mom was looking at." He points to a row of peach boxes.

It's at the end of the aisle I need, so I slip past and grab the pills. When I return, he's still standing in front of the perfume. "Do you need some?" I joke.

"Ha, ha." His fake laugh is intentionally flat, and he turns and follows me to the check out.

"Mission accomplished." I pay for my items and lead the way out the door. "Now, grab your candy so we can go eat."

Rigsby feeds my dollars into the vending machine. He has the code for his favorite candy memorized and punches it in. As soon as the machine drops his candy, he grabs it and we leave, heading to our favorite spot to eat.

At Red Barn, the hostess recognizes us. "How's it going today?" she asks as she gathers silverware and menus.

"We're doing okay." I take a step forward and look around. The place is busy with many of the tables filled with people wearing Granite Ice jerseys. More than likely, after the game was canceled, they all went out. My chest tightens at the mere thought of it all, but I know better than to spend too much time dwelling on it. I push the thought out of my head and glance at the hostess to see what's taking her so long.

"Are your wife and daughter joining you tonight or is it just the boys again?" She's staring at me, but I toss a look over my shoulder to see who she is actually talking to. Nobody is behind me. I sputter out a cough. This is the second time someone thought Kaci was my wife. It's like the universe is mocking me. I've never been asked before if anyone was my wife, let alone twice in two days.

"It's just us." I jerk my thumb to Rigsby. To avoid being asked that question a third time, I take the time to clarify things. "I'm not married. That woman was just a friend."

"Too bad. You two would make an adorable couple." She quirks a brow like she knows something I don't before walking forward. I'm left struggling to make my legs work.

Why does that affect me so much?

Kaci is gorgeous. Yes, we could make a cute couple, but she made it clear she wasn't interested in dating. So it doesn't matter that we'd be a cute couple.

I stumble forward with Rigsby by my side. When we get to our booth, we slide in, and order our wings and root beer. Since it's wing night, everything comes quickly, and Rigsby eagerly reaches into the bucket, not shy about pulling out the biggest one.

It makes me smile at how comfortable he is with me. I survey the wings, deliberately avoiding the big ones so he can have them and settle on the runt. "Thanks for not bringing Frankfurter to the game tonight." I grin through my first bite and ask, "Is he still living in your backpack?"

"No, I only had him in there for your house. He's in a cage in my closet." He draws in a breath and then blows it out with a small shake of his head. "Thanks for not telling my mom about him."

"Your secret is safe with me—for now, but maybe we can tell her together. She might not be as upset as you think and keeping him in a cage in the closet doesn't sound like the best life. He needs to get out more."

I grab my drink and take a long sip. It's odd but it almost feels like something is missing from this meal.

And it's not the food.

The wings are amazing as always. I just keep looking around, like I'm expecting someone else to be there, which is insane because I have been single forever. I eat alone all the time. Rigsby's company should feel like a lot compared to what I'm used to.

I grab another wing and chew off the skin with force.

"Are you mad about the game?" Rigsby reaches across the table and takes the last wing in the bucket. "You're quiet."

"I don't think so." I've developed some sort of nervous fidget, scratching the back of my head. Not because it itches, but because sitting here is a struggle.

Rigsby props his elbow on the table and leans over. "You should have gotten Kaci the perfume I told you about, Mr. Rizzard of Oz."

"Excuse me?" I do a double take. Where did that come from? "What do you know about rizz? You're seven."

"I know you don't have enough, because it's all over your face that you like Kaci."

"No, it's not." I straighten up, trying to hold a serious expression. "It's not on there."

"Uncle Jack." He gives me the most pointed stare I've ever seen from a kid. "Bella and I saw you kiss her."

"You did?" I scratch my head again. This conversation seems a little too mature to be having with Rigsby. Before I can change the subject he goes on.

"Bella said that it was a huge mistake to kiss her mom."

"Oh. Really?"

"Yeah, her mom says she'll get a man when pigs learn to fly."

Okay, that makes me chuckle. I can see Kaci saying that, especially to Bella. Trying to explain the complexities of human relationships to a child is just too hard and keeping it funny is definitely the way to go. I don't get why she's so guarded. I haven't given her a reason not to trust me. All I want is a chance to get to know her. I'm not asking her to get married. I just want to go roller blading or something...

Now, I'm really unsettled.

Something is missing from this dinner, and I know what it is.

The problem is that she's not going to believe I'm serious. She's not going to believe any words at all. She needs me to show her that I'm not looking for a distraction. If I'm going to let someone into my life now, it'll only be because I'm ready to make her my everything.

I have to find a way to show her that.

The sooner the better—because if I wait too long, it'll only make her doubt me more.

Yanking my wallet out of my jacket pocket, I thumb through the cash until I find what I need, tossing it in the center of the table. I rise to my feet and jerk my head toward the exit behind me. "Let's go, Rigsby. We have work to do."

"What are we doing?" He slides off his seat, lowering his brow into a perplexed position.

"I'm not sure yet." I dig in my pocket for my keys, knowing whatever it is, it's bound to be something big. Then, to make Rigsby laugh (because I love his laugh) I say, "Let's just say, oink oink. Time for pigs to fly."

Seventeen

I peek my head into Bella's bedroom and hold my breath. She looks so peaceful with the soft moonlight from her window shining on her cheek. Her shoulder slowly moves up and down with her breath. I don't think I'll ever get used to seeing Little B 2, sleeping in her arms, but I'm so glad she isn't sad about losing Little B. I slip my foot back, closing the door as I make my exit, but Bella startles and turns toward me. "Mom?"

Oh no! I should not have bothered her.

"I didn't mean to wake you," I whisper, taking yet another step backwards. "Go back to sleep."

"I wasn't sleeping." She shuffles under her blanket and pushes to a half-seated position. "What did you want?"

"Nothing, baby," I drop my volume even more. "I was just checking on you. Go back to sleep. School tomorrow." Bella lies back down but doesn't stay quiet.

"Are you sad about Jackson?"

"I'm not sad," my rebuttal is instant and snappy. "Why would you think that?" I hold up a finger, tapping a spot in the air as if pointing to him, while adding, "I don't even know him."

"I saw you kiss him." Her random admission hits me with so much force that I gulp.

"You saw that?" My breath quickens, it hadn't dawned on me that the kids have witnessed that. The last thing I need is for her to end up confused—or worse yet, thinking there's something going on between us. "It didn't mean anything," I rush out. "You don't need to worry about me and Jackson." My voice grows high-pitched, as if it's the most absurd thing ever to say aloud.

She turns her head from me. Even in the darkened room, I can make out the serious lines on her face. From the straight lips to angled-down brows, she's worrying again. "Baby." I cross the room until I make it to her bedside. "Sometimes things happen, and they aren't what you plan on, or what you want." I lean over, brush the tips of my fingers through her hair, smoothing it out of her face. I add, "Jackson kissed me, and it wasn't anything I was expecting. We talked about it, and we both know it was a total fluke. It will never happen again. You don't have to worry about it."

Instead of her lips tipping into a contented grin, her serious lines deepen. It's quite evident she's scowling. "Baby," I swipe the last strand of hair from her cheek and tuck it behind her ear. "Please don't be upset. It wasn't anything I planned on, and it doesn't change anything."

"Why not?" She sits up and most of the hair I had neatly tucked behind her spills over her shoulder again.

"What do you mean? Why not?" Bella is rarely confrontational about anything. She's the most obedient and agreeable child who

ever existed. Where is this fear coming from? A wave of guilt floods
my gut for missing her concern. All I want to do is assure her that
nothing's changed, and she has nothing to worry about. I try again.
"Because I won't let it change anything."

"Don't you see?" There's a warning branded into her tone.
"When you look at Jackson, you actually smile. That kiss made
you happy." The next words trickle out as a plea. "Why would you
push that away?"

Shock and a rush of astonishment, mixed with shots of adrenaline, fire through my veins. Bella has never said anything about this
before—I had no idea she sensed my unhappiness. The last thing
I need is another reason to feel mom guilt.

I pushed Jackson away because he couldn't possibly be interested in me for anything more than just random flirting; I only
attract losers. When he figures out that he's too good for me, he'll
leave. There's no Prince Charming waiting for me, but Bella is only
seven. She wants to believe in the fairy tale happily-ever-afters. I
hate to break her heart. How do I tell her that fairytales aren't real?
Or that there is no way a guy like Jackson could end up wanting to
date me seriously.

Bella's eyes twinkle with hope-filled specs, but all it does is flood
my stomach with more guilt. "Well," I begin, fully aware that she's
only seven. I'll never be the mom who parentifies her daughter.
Some things she doesn't need to understand—at least not yet. "I
was smiling so much because I was watching you smile while you
played with Rigsby."

I pause, as that was exceptionally hard to force over the new
lump in my throat. I'm not one to get choked up, as communi-

cation isn't hard for me, but my body knows when I'm not being completely honest.

Maybe it's a liar's lump?

I'm not trying to deceive her, but she doesn't need to sit here hopeful for something that isn't going to happen.

Her lips turn down even more, taking my heart with it. "Last summer when we went to visit Grandma, she said you don't think you deserve to be loved."

"Why would Grandma say that?" I practically growl. Sometimes my mom says the rudest things. My defensiveness rises, and I blurt out, "Trust me, Bella. I want us to be happy. If I ever get a real chance at love, I'm not going to push it away, but that kiss—" My voice cracks, and I clear my throat. "That kiss was just a kiss." I place my hand on her arm and give it a playful squeeze. "And you're seven and should never worry about that. Or me. It's my job to do all the worrying. You just be seven." To end the conversation on a high note, I pat her pillow. "Time to rest."

She's slow to lower herself back down, but her sleepiness is evident by how quickly she closes her eyes. I lean over, sweeping her hair out of her face one more time and press a kiss to her forehead. I pause for a beat, notice how her breathing has already begun to deepen. Then, on the tips of my toes, I quickly slip out, holding my breath until the door clicks softly shut behind me.

A sigh of relief slips from my lips as my gaze finds the clock on the microwave. Almost nine. I could totally go to bed early, and crash out, but I need to finish reading for class. On my way to the kitchen, I grab my books from the entryway, and plop down at the table. Thanks to my unpaid electric bill marking the page, my book opens right up to where I left off. Setting the bill aside, I make a mental note to pay it on Friday. I scan the last section to remember what this chapter is even about, but my memory isn't jogged, so I move back to another section.

Tap. Tap.

It's awfully late to have someone drop by. My first instinct is to grab my phone and check for a text. Nothing. I don't want the knocking to wake Bella, and I quickly move to the door and look through the peep hole.

My heart cinches tight in my chest, and my breathing becomes unstable.

Cracking the door open, I peek through the gap.

"Hey." Jackson shifts from one foot to the other and slides his gaze down to Rigsby, who beams back at me.

"I'm fresh out of lucky gloves," I manage to say with a straight face.

His jaw drops in an exaggerated shock, clearly caught off guard by my quick wit. His expression shifts to one that's more stoic and he draws my attention to a sack he's holding. "I ah, brought Bella something."

"You did?" I stare at it suspiciously, as if poisonous gas is wafting from the sack.

What is happening?

Why is he even here?

And bringing gifts.

I was able to resist his charm once.

That was hard enough.

He can't just show up unannounced and flash that flirty smirk. "It will only take a second." He respectfully drops his voice in volume. "Can we come in just for a minute?"

I toss a look behind me. To my surprise, Bella's door is not closed. Her tiny button nose is pressed in the crack. "Why not?" Giving up, I fling the door open, and I raise my volume to an exaggerated level to make sure Bella can hear me. "You can stay for as long as it takes us to have one drink."

Bella's door flies open, strolling right up to Jackson without a hint of shyness. "Just the girl I wanted to see," Jackson says, bending to eye level and tips the top of the sack toward her. "Reach in here and grab your present."

Her eyes flutter with excitement, and a giggle escapes as she reaches into the sack. The moment her fingers make contact, her eyebrows rocket to the ceiling, and she lets out a delighted squeal. When she pulls her hand back, she has Little B.

My head snaps back as my gaze narrows in disbelief. I picture Jackson going to the cemetery, but I quickly reject the notion. "You did not."

"It wasn't so bad, right?" Jackson elbows Rigsby. The way he pinches his lips back, and Rigsby fills in the silence with nervous chuckles, makes me shake my head.

"I can't believe it." I'm surprised how even my tone is, since I suddenly feel breathless.

"Can we go play, Mom?" Bella tightly squeezes Little B to her chest. "I need to introduce Little B to her sister." I force myself to ignore how many germs the bear must have collected after spending a night outside. I'll wash her in the morning. Now is the time for a joyful reunion. Holding up both of my hands, I flash ten digits. "Ten minutes."

She waves Rigsby forward, and they scurry off. I take a second to stare after them before returning my gaze to Jackson. With my heart hammering in my chest, I utter. "Come in."

My legs teeter as I shut the door behind him and cross to the small kitchen to the coffee pot. He takes a seat at the table and watches me. There's cold coffee resting in the bottom of the pot, and I take what's left, divide it into two cups, and place the mugs in the microwave. "It's not coffee shop quality," I joke when I place one in front of him on the table.

"It's perfect." He picks up his mug and motions to the seat across from him. "You need to sit. I didn't come over here for you to wait on me."

I retrieve my mug and lower myself into the chair. Jackson leans forward, resting his forearms on the table. I notice he's wearing another Granite Ice hoodie. It seems to be the only thing he wears, but I'm not complaining. Before I can stop myself, I visualize borrowing those oversized sweatshirts and forgetting to give them back. I stare at the sleeve. It's the perfect shade of navy and made of fleece that looks so soft I could get lost in it. Heat creeps in my chest.

Phew. Stop it. I am not catching feelings for this guy!

"I'm still amazed you went to get that bear. I love Bella with all my heart, but even I wasn't going to crawl down there."

"It wasn't too bad." He jerks his thumb toward the door behind him. "At least not with Rigsby to talk to. I wouldn't have wanted to go there alone. I was surprised to see they hadn't closed the grave, and the bear was right on top."

I frown in contemplation. "I sing at funerals pretty regularly, but I never paid much attention to how the process works. It's sort of rare for me to go to the graveyard." Goosebumps ripple up my spine, spooking me to sit straight up. I declare, "Okay, new subject. I don't need to visualize you traipsing around there at night. I won't sleep for a week."

"What do you want to talk about?" His puckish smile loosens something in me. Most of my everyday interactions are concise and serious. Everything in that smile says, "It's okay to be playful," and before I think of anything normal, I bleep out, "Well, what is your death row meal?"

One of his brow's spikes, and a chuckle leaks out of his mouth. "I thought you wanted to get away from the morbid?"

"It's not morbid. It's a serious question." I cup my hands around my mug, soaking in the warm glow that seeps to my hands, and plunge into all my options. "So, all-you-can-eat pizza would be top on my list, because why limit volume if you're on your way out. If calories aren't a concern, how about just like a whole chocolate cake? Or maybe it's better to try something new? Something exotic that I've never tried. It's a lot to think about." I gesture forward. "Your turn—and beware there are wrong answers."

"Wrong answers?" He starts to say something and then stops, tipping his chin up, all while the mischievous smile pulls on the corners of his lips. "There cannot be wrong answers if it's death row."

"Oh, yeah, there are," I barrel on. "Anything people eat for the sake of health. Like salad. That's a wrong answer."

His bottom lip pushes out a tad farther than the top one, making it look extra plump while he thinks. I wait; my brain is ready to calculate if we are compatible. He raises his coffee mug, pressing the edge to his lips, and says, "mac and cheese," before taking a sip.

"What?" I exclaim, feigning outrage. "Of all the things you could have. You could have a giant steak, and you pick macaroni and cheese?"

He bops his head and takes another sip of his coffee before setting it down. "Yeah, it's the ultimate comfort food. Of course, I wouldn't just accept the one from the box. I want my mother's homemade recipe—the one with real cheese."

He's got me there. Food mixed with family traditions and comfort. "Alright," I groan. "You pass."

"My turn to ask a question." He raises his mug, gesturing with it. His eyes narrow. Then, with the poutiest of lips, he declares, "First kiss."

"Kiss?" Sputtering, I narrowly miss choking on my coffee. "We're talking about kissing?" Those full lips of his hit me like a truck. That's it. I'm done. He could ask for my social security number and my birth certificate, and I'd gladly hand them over. "Ah, would you believe me if I said it was you?" I squawk out, hoping my joke will mask how cowardly I feel.

Instead of laughing, he arches an eyebrow in a suggestive slant. "Did that kiss make you uncomfortable?"

"Uncomfortable?" I echo while a bomb explodes in my chest. That's the last word I would use to describe what happened. *That kiss made me feel a lot of things but not discomfort. Wanted. Beautiful. Cared for. All amazing feelings I haven't experienced in years, but there's no way I can admit that.*

While I ponder what to say, he drags his teeth slowly over the perfect bottom lip while his gaze roves over my face, moving from my lips to my eyes. I clench my hands into fists, resisting the urge to point at him and scream how that's not fair.

This whole thing is a setup!

He can't come waltzing over here all hours of the night and return my daughter's most prized possession—*that he raised from the dead*—and act as if it's not a big deal to sit here and talk kissing with me casually while looking like that! I hold in all my words but manage a sharp shake of my head. Eventually, "I didn't say uncomfortable," tumbles out of my mouth.

"Well, at least you're not salty about it." A flirty laugh drips from those perfect lips. "I couldn't help but think I ruined my chance with you because I pushed too fast." His tone is pure seriousness, as he goes on, "But you have to know I was nervous about not getting another chance to see you."

The deep ache that hits my gut way down in the pit, causes me to place my hand on my stomach. I'm not cut out for this flirting stuff.

The last of my defensive line makes its stand: I'm too fragile. It's too risky. I will run over hot glass Legos, before I trust another man. It's one thing if it was just me, but Bella has already suffered enough from my terrible choices.

Frankly, I already explained this to him the other day. A single bubble of anger blooms in my gut. Before I can overthink it, I blurt out, "Who do you think you are?

"You won't even find out if you won't let me in."

Every fold of my brain absorbs his words, and it sends a shock-wave directly to my heart. "How can you be so sure about this when we only just met?"

"It's just a vibe. Sure, we haven't known each other long, but this feels different. I like everything about you so far." He shrugs, casually, shifting the angle of his broad shoulders closer to me, while his gaze softens. "Earlier at the store, Rigsby showed me this perfume you had wanted. He told me I should get it for you, but it was honestly the most absurd thing to me. I wouldn't ever want to change the way you smell."

"Say what?" My bottom lip quivers. How am I having another conversation about my smell? Locking my jaws together, I refuse to show my anxiety. I get it. I'm not perfect, but it's not for lack of trying. I'm maxed out. My breathing is unsteady when I ask, "You noticed my smell?"

His nod is instant, unapologetic, and it sends a dagger to my heart until he tacks on, "Yeah, I told you that you smelled great."

I slant my head, unsure I heard that correctly. A warm glow seeps into my chest, as if it's healing an open wound. I draw in a breath, press my lips together, and look at him. I really look at him, raking my gaze over his deep-set eyes, all the way down to that superior jaw line. It's a face I have memorized, but it feels different to look at him now. Like I've unlocked another layer—*a soft one.* One that I'm compelled to explore.

I blink and then blink again. He has one little wispy strand of hair that dangles in front of his eyes. It's likely caused by a cowlick, but the way it shadows his gaze makes him extra dreamy. I don't know how long I can keep making excuses, especially if he's going to keep coming back stronger.

"It's just the little things like that." He stretches an arm over his head and slouches back in his chair, an impish smile on his face.

Does he know what he's doing when he hits me with that smile? It's like the brightest light that I've been missing for so long, after wandering through darkness for years.

"Look," he pushes his chair back but leans forward, directing his gaze at me. "I get it now; that kiss was too impulsive. I got caught up in the moment, but I want to get to know you more."

I inhale sharply and adrenaline surges through my veins. My heart pounds in my chest. Memories flash through my brain. All the years I begged Chase to want me and to want to fight for us and realizing he never cared about anything but himself. And now, here's a man who's intentional with his words, willing to fight for something. Neither one of us even knows what it is and all I've done is push him away.

The truth of the matter is, the kiss wasn't wrong. It didn't bother me in the way he thinks. It bothered me because it awakened a feeling for him that I was unwilling to feel. I was unwilling to feel it because I didn't think it was genuine.

But now...

I can, maybe, possibly, be swayed to think differently.

Neither one of us speaks as our eyes lock, dialing into one another, and it's like we are meeting in a new dimension. After a beat of the loudest silence ever, he slides his hand across the table and places it on top of mine. I melt into the table. I wouldn't be able to curl my fingers into his if I tried, because my palm is nothing but goo.

With a gentle squeeze of my hand, he enacts some magnetic force that pulls me to him, and in unison, we move closer together.

It's slow.

Intentional.

The opposite of last time.

I tip up my chin, watching him watch me. His attention is unwavering as we pause, mere inches from each other. I study his expression, drinking in the warmth that permeates from his skin. His finger finds my chin, and with the faintest touch, tips it a little more. In the lowest speed setting, he brushes his bottom lip against mine, and goosebumps spiral up my spine.

Giggles erupt behind us.

Jackson presses a smile into our kiss before we break away, turning to peer at our audience hovering in Bella's doorway.

"Shows over." Jackson stands up, waves Rigsby forward. "We really do need to get you back home." He takes a step toward the door and gives me a playful side-eye. "I'm going to text you when I get home. If that's okay."

I look at Bella, who's still peeking out from behind her door. Her face is glowing in a way I don't think I've ever seen before. When I glance back at Jackson, his eyes reflect the same glow back at me. I don't feel anything other than peace. This time it's perfect.

The fear I felt before is gone.

"Sure." My lips pull into a genuine smile. The tug is so strong I have to force myself to keep it modest. "I look forward to it."

Rigsby tugs at Jackson's sleeve, pulling him closer to the door, and I lift my hand in a silent wave, my eyes lingering on Rigsby's hold on that sweatshirt.

It's a nice sweatshirt.

I have a feeling I'm going to be borrowing that very soon.

Eighteen

Taking a deep breath, I hold it as I stand in the gymnasium doorway, scanning the hordes of people. *Where is he?*

Chase said he'd be here, *stressing he was leaving band practice early,* like he had to let me know what a bother this was to him. I'll believe him when I see him.

I came prepared with a purse full of clean tissues and money for all the games, but in a perfect world, he shows up for Bella.

"Do you see Dad?" Bella stands on the tips of her toes, straining her neck. Her pupils are dilated, and quick breathes rush in and out of her mouth.

"Well..." At this point, I'm checking all the faces. Those with hats, and others with bald heads, even though Chase has a full head of air. We don't need another huge disappointment this week. This is Bella's school festival, the most popular family night. All the kids come with their parents. As much as I despise Chase, I'm willing to put our co-parenting to the test for Bella. That is...if he shows up. I release my breath slowly and turn toward her. "He might be running a little late. He did say he had something to do. Why don't we try a round at the candy wheel while we wait?"

Her smile—which had been so full—deflates like a popped balloon. "I'd rather wait here, so he can find me."

Nervous bubbles fizzle through my stomach, and I glance over my other shoulder. It's times like these I have the hardest time biting my tongue. We could have a lovely time, just the two of us. Instead, I'm standing here, holding onto the hope that he won't ruin our entire night. "Kaci," a strong baritone voice calls from behind me. Bella and I pivot at the same time, but she beats me to the hello.

"Rigsby!"

A confused chuckle breaks past my lips as Jackson and Rigsby approach us. I'm beginning to think Jackson's kidnapped Rigsby because he has him all the time. It pulls at my heartstrings to see someone who's not even this kid's dad show up time and time again. "Babysitting again?"

Jackson's easy grin finds me, and he maintains eye contact. "I'm trying to do my part to help out with the new baby. Tom had a work meeting, and Jackie didn't want to bring the baby out with all these germs. It's only for an hour anyway." He jerks his thumb over his shoulder toward the games. "Do you guys want a shot at the candy wheel?"

Bella's gaze slams back to the entrance, her cheeks a rosy hue. "Ah, you guys can go ahead." I gesture. "We are waiting for Bella's dad. It's his night with her, and he should be here any minute."

"Oh, okay." Jackson says casually as Rigsby snatches his wrist, attempting to drag him forward. "We'll be around for a while if you change your mind."

"Sounds good." Bella's hyper focused on the door, and I can't stop watching her. Every hard swallow hits me right in my mama heart.

"Is it okay if I text you later?" Jackson digs his heel in, holding Rigsby while he adds, "I was going to try to get ahold of you anyway."

"Sure." I'm quieter than normal. I hate to make plans, because when it comes to Chase, I never know what's going on.

"Hurry, the candy wheel is filling up," Rigsby insists, giving Jackson another tug. They both go flying forward. Laughter rushes as Jackson's jaw drops into an expression seeped in happiness. I'm left frozen, staring at his giant smile.

I never really thought about the kind of man I wanted to father my kid before it happened. I was young, dumb, and so naïve. Seeing Jackson willing to be dragged around an elementary school gymnasium by a seven-year-old—who isn't even his child—sort of makes me feel like I've been missing out on something. Every second I spent with Chase, he carried himself like he was doing us a favor.

"Do you think he forgot?" Bella's expression is so strained, a blue vein by her temple—that I'd hardly noticed before—thickens. Maybe it's just me, but I don't think seven-year-olds should have stress veins.

Placing my hand behind her back, I'm gentle as I pull her close. Her feet are cemented to the spot, and she's not moving. "Baby, let's go play a few games. As soon as he gets here, we'll meet up."

Before she can reply, a small crowd of kids pass behind us, all laughing and smiling as if it's the best day ever. Bella looks at them, and her lips tighten. I run my hands through my hair. Maybe it's a bad idea to wait inside. I search for the exit. Standing here, is just making her see all the fun she's missing out on. She won't participate until her dad is here, and once again, he's not here. I'm so white-hot with anger that I force my limbs to freeze, afraid I might throw some sort of a fit. It's one thing to be late for a child transfer, but this is at her school and in front of her friends. *She doesn't deserve this.* "Baby," I try again, but I'm weary because I know she's not going to enjoy herself, even if I can distract her with a game.

"Bella!" Rigsby jogs up beside her, his arms filled with at least a dozen king-sized boxes of candy. "I won the jackpot!"

She pulls her gaze from the exit and studies his loot. He's got gummies, chocolate, and sour candies. Jackson stands back, as if purposely keeping his distance, but I'm grateful for the distraction. Anything to get Bella to stop staring at the door.

"What kind do you want?" Rigsby goes on, fanning them out for her to see. She steps forward, and a tiny curve tips on the edge of her lips as she grabs a box of chocolates. She starts to turn back to the door, but Rigsby beckons her. "Come on! You have to try it. You could win all this."

His smile fills his whole face. I hold my breath, hoping she takes the bait. Anything to take her mind off Chase. She glances at the door for a fast moment before looking at me. "Can I go Mom?"

"Yeah." I give my largest nod. "Of course. Let's win some candy." I'm already moving, not taking a chance to lose this momentum. Bella takes small steps, but they are in the right direction. Rigsby hangs by her side, pumping her up the whole way over to the candy wheel. I hastily dig in my purse for some dollar bills and press them into her palm. Rigsby takes Bella to the front of the line, and I stand back, watching it all unfold. She's smiling. Not a big grin, but it's genuine when she selects her number.

I let out a sigh of relief. The hard part is over. Now that she's playing games, we have something to do to pass the time. Chase will eventually show up. He always comes when it's convenient for him.

Jackson moves to stand next to me, his face expressionless and he says, "I didn't know if I should come over, but Rigsby couldn't handle seeing her so sad. I hope we aren't making it worse."

"No." I adjust my purse higher on my shoulder, which seems so much heavier than normal. "I appreciate it. Sometimes I don't know what to do. He'll come eventually, and this will keep her from crying." My eyes sweep across the gym again. I just can't believe he's this late. Wait, no, I can believe it. I'm just disgusted. I slope my gaze back to Jackson, standing solid without even a fidget, like he's happy to be here. There's something to be said for men like Jackson. I mean, truly I barely know him, but he's at a school carnival for a kid who isn't even his. "How's the new baby anyway?" I ask.

"Good." He lifts a shoulder. "Not that I know anything about babies, but everything seems to be normal. The parents are tired. The baby has his days and nights mixed up, but I hear that happens. The laundry is piling up."

"Yeah." It's my turn to shake my head as I remember those days all too well. "That sounds normal."

"Dad!" Bella's shrill cry of happiness slices through the air. I pivot. My heart actually crawls all the way up my throat. Chase looks as if he just crawled out of bed, wearing dirty jeans, and a T-shirt.

But he's here.

Bella runs over, and smashes into him. It stings that instead of bending over and scooping her up into the biggest hug, he stands there, merely reaching out and ruffling her hair while she holds a death grip on his leg. It's moments like these where I have this super ability to let all the background noise fade, and all I see is her beautiful smile. He's listening to her talk, or at least doing a good job at pretending to listen, as she proceeds to pull him to the candy wheel.

I swallow back my disgust and watch them pick a number. He doesn't even reach into his wallet. Instead, he points to the few dollars she's still holding from the ones I gave her. She puts one down on the counter, beaming a smile up at him.

This is not the life I wanted for her.

Jackson's soft words pull me out of my trance. "I kind of feel like Rigsby's intruding on Bella's time with her dad. I can grab him."

"Oh no. He's perfectly fine there." I wave my hand, dismissing his concern. "Chase will care more that I'm here. I should actually be on my way. Now that he's here, they'll be fine. I wouldn't like it if he loitered on my time."

Jackson twists his wrist, peeking at his watch. "Well, we've already been here an hour. I think I'll give Rigsby a last call and get him home. I don't want to barge in too late and risk destroying the bedtime routine for the new baby."

I snort a warning. "The baby is only a few days old. Trust me, there's no routine yet."

"Right." He chuckles in agreement. "It looks like you might have the night off then. Do you want to grab a late dinner?"

He's looking at me in a new way no guy has with an urgency that makes my heart swell. Food always sounds amazing, but a dinner date with Jackson? That is a glorious thought. "I'd like that."

"Perfect." His easy grin shows off his perfectly even teeth, and he jerks his thumb over his shoulder, tacking on, "I'll get Rigsby home and text you."

I nod, letting my top teeth sink into my bottom lip as I struggle to hold back my excitement. "Sounds perfect."

Nineteen

JACKSON

I stand outside Kaci's door, shifting my weight from one leg to the other. When she opens the door, I inhale sharply. She's wearing her hair down in soft waves that fall almost to the middle of her back, and a dark navy sweater paired with jeans. All the blue highlights the different hues in her eyes. She's absolutely stunning.

"Our first official date." I forgo a traditional hello. "How do you feel?"

"I'm ready." A playful smile tugs on her lips as she pulls the door open wide, her eyes glittering when she says, "Come on in."

"Thanks for having me over." I slip inside. This is the hard part of the night. The awkwardness. It's our first date. In a strange way, I feel as if we've already had about five dates. I want our first real date to be special and memorable. She's all I've thought about, and I couldn't wait to see her again. Oddly when I offered to take her out to eat, she said she didn't feel like going out and offered to eat dinner here. I hold up my takeout bag from The Grove, the place she actually works as she offered to call in a to-go order. "I got our food."

She brushes her hand across her midsection. "It smells amazing, and I'm starving."

I walk to the table, remove her salad from the bag, and hand it to her. "No onions or tomatoes. Just as you requested."

"Thank you." She places it on the table and sits down, taking a minute to stare at me. I don't think I'll ever get used to the way it feels to have her look at me. I set my to-go box in front of my chair and pause, returning her gaze. She goes on staring for another couple of seconds before she lowers her head, and says, "Thank you for understanding about me not wanting to go out. I hope that didn't upset you."

"No, not at all." I say, shaking my head before opening my box, giving my burger a good whiff. It smells amazing. "I'm happy to do whatever you want."

"Yeah, after the week we both had, I was just ready to be home and not run around." She scoots her chair forward, grabs her fork and digs in. "Plus, since I work in food service, I prefer to just be home when I'm not at work."

"I completely understand that." She's happily munching on her salad, but I can't take my eyes off her. "I travel so much for hockey that I love a night in."

"I'm glad we have that in common." Her eyes glow with the warmth of a sunset in heaven, drawing me deeper into their depth. "So, I wanted to bring up a weird text I got from Chase."

"Oh." Heat flames my cheeks, as I have a sense of what she's about to say. "Everything okay?"

"This is going to seem sort of out there, but did you say something to him?"

"Did I say something to your ex?" I glance down at my burger and then raise my attention back to her. "He's an idiot."

"I already know that, and learned that the hard way," she scoffs, setting her fork down, continuing, "You told him he was an idiot?"

"Not in so many words." I tilt my head back, mulling over how much I want to disclose. I don't want to waste our time talking about her loser ex, but she needs to know that I said something. Leaning back, I wipe my mouth with a napkin and drop it back to my lap. "Look, I went over to grab Rigsby. He asked what my deal was and how our kids got connected."

Her lips part, as if she's holding back saying something. It's so hard to sit here with her looking at me like that, all vulnerable. I reach across the table, take her hand in mine, and everything spews out, "Look, maybe it was forward of me. I'm not one of those guys with a temper that you have to worry about, but I wasn't going to beat around the bush. I let him know who I was and that I was getting to know you and Bella. He seemed taken aback by it, started to blubber something, and I sort of just lost it on him."

"Did you threaten him?" Her lips press together. I'm not sure if that means she's happy or mad.

"Look, I just had a concern about how he was treating you. I know you aren't together, but that doesn't mean he doesn't have to respect you. You're still the mother of his child." I nod and add, "I took care of my concern."

"I didn't ask you to do that," she says, her words slow. She leans forward, her hair spilling over her shoulder, framing her face in the most perfect way.

"No, you didn't." I don't decipher a warning in her words, and I'm not going to lie. "I'm not going to apologize for it. Maybe it seemed a little soon to cross that boundary, but I didn't think so. I'm planning to spend a lot of time with you and Bella, and she is his daughter." I'm not one to pour my heart out. It's not what I do, but I do stand up for what is right and for the people I care about. "He has a right to know who I am and my intentions."

"Your intentions?" A sly smile sprouts on her lips as she pins her gaze on me.

"My intentions." I hear her echo as a challenge. My jaw locks and I stare, my muscles twitching, urging me to be honest. I don't know any other way to say it than to be honest, and I reach my free hand out to cup her cheek. "I'm going to treat you like the queen you are. That means if anyone else is disrespecting you, Chase included, I'm stopping it. I'm not about violence. I'm just all about you."

Her sly smile fades, making my breath quicken. Neither of us speaks. It's like sudden death, the tension so thick, it's nearly boiling over. My heart rams so hard against my chest, I'm at the point where I will ramble nonsense if I open my mouth. I said what I needed to say. Now I wait for her to respond.

She raises her hand up, covering my hand that still rests on her cheek. Her skin is satiny, soft and smooth, and it causes my breath to hitch in my chest. All I want to do is lean over and kiss her, but she's so still, I freeze too.

"Tell me what that means," she whispers, "to be all about me."

"It means, I want to memorize every smile you have. I want to sit at this table with you and eat cold take out, talking for hours about anything and everything. I want to look up and see you in the hockey stands during my games. I'm not going to make any promises I don't intend to keep. Maybe that's not enough, and I know we just met each other, but I can't stop thinking about you. I don't know what that means, but I want to find out."

She's quiet, but her eyes fill with longing, and I know that look. It's the one she gave me last night before I kissed her, and I'm no fool.

I slide my hand down her neck, curling my fingers to pull her close. She doesn't resist. Her eyes flutter shut right as my lips capture hers. I lean forward, dragging my lips slowly over hers, wanting to consume her with all my senses. Inhaling, I drink in her scent—indescribable. Addicting, yet subtle. I can't get enough of it, and I'm left breathless as I pull away before our kiss turns to anything more than sweet.

A breath shudders out of her as she stares back at me. I'm still holding her hand, and I raise it to my lips and press a chaste kiss to her knuckles, letting my lips linger for just a few seconds. None of this makes sense, but at the same time, I don't care.

Epilogue

A Year Later

"Did you think I forgot about you?" Jackson says as soon as I open the door. It's an hour after a home game, and no one is celebrating because it was another loss. Surprisingly, he's actually grinning.

"I know you didn't forget." I rise to the tips of my toes and tilt my chin up, pressing a chaste hello-kiss to his lips. "I'm used to the insane amount of time it takes you to remove all your gear. And double-check for your glove eighteen times." I open the door wider, stepping to the side so he can enter. "Did you guys go out?"

"No." He slips his shoes off, setting them neatly next to mine. "I was in a hurry to get over here. I knew if I didn't, you'd be sleeping by ten."

I laugh because it's true. It's Chase's night to have Bella, and I'm exhausted. I graduated last spring without a job offer, so I started substitute teaching this fall. Every day it's a different classroom, with a new set of kids, a new set of rules. It's enough to make my head explode. By the time Friday rolls around, I'm ready to fall face first onto the couch and go into a coma. "Sorry about your game." I take the to-go bag from his hands and drop it on the center of the table.

We are the biggest homebodies on the planet, and we've developed the most basic routines—routines that are consumed completely in each other. I can't help but think I'm the luckiest woman. I don't need fancy dinners or dates. Just someone to share my time with.

Someone who gets me.

That Jackson does.

It's never just the bare minimum with him. He spoils me with the little things, like date nights at my place when I can't stand to be in public. He always shows up for me and Bella, taking care of the little things—even the big things, like when he spoke to Chase about showing me more respect. I wouldn't have believed it if I hadn't seen it, but having Jackson around has made Chase more punctual with his time with Bella. It might be in my head, but Chase even seems a little more attentive when they are together. It's not a miracle by any means, but it's progress.

Jackson drops into the chair that Bella now refers to as "Jackson's spot" and takes his burger out of the to-go box. "How was teaching today?"

"Good." My eyes are heavy, but my heart is full as I shift my face to his. It's a lot to sub every day, but I love it. "I was in sixth grade today. So, the fractions were fractioning a little hard for a Friday. I had a couple extra cups of coffee, but I made it through."

"I hate when fractions fraction too much." His smile is easy, and I notice his facial hair is shorter than normal. Usually he keeps it scruffy, often going several days without shaving. I don't prefer it one way or the other. I enjoy never knowing what I'm getting.

I smile, watching as his eyes bounce from my lips to my eyes. His lips move as if about to say something, but then he sighs and drops his attention back to his burger.

"Everything okay?" His lips are set into a bit of a grim line, and I can't help but think something is off.

"Fine." His brows pinch as his gaze drops to my shirt. "I was looking for that sweatshirt for like an hour this morning."

"This sweatshirt?" I playfully bat my lashes and pull the hooded collar tighter around my neck. "I might have swiped it from your hamper the other day."

"You don't have to steal my dirty laundry." He tips his forehead closer. "I can get you a clean one."

"I love the ones that smell like you." I laugh, shrugging. "Plus, I know how to do laundry. If I wanted it to be clean, I would wash it."

A soft laugh gusts from his chest as his eyes latch onto mine with intensity. "I know you know how to do laundry. Remember?"

"Oh yes." I throw my head back laughing, thinking back to meeting him at the laundromat. I had no idea what I'd really found that day when I picked up that glove—but if I've learned anything about Jackson the last year, it's that he's obsessed with it. He never lets it out of his sight. I'm still waiting for the "luck" to kick in though, because the team is on a losing streak. I sigh, adding, "I'll never forget your lucky glove."

"You can't say it's not your lucky glove too." He leans back, pointing a finger toward me.

"Mine?" My face must have been colored with confusion, because we both know that even after months of going to games, I know very little about hockey.

"Well, yeah." He reaches across the table, taking my hand and threading his fingers into mine. "It brought us together."

"That's true." I sigh again, this time leaning forward as his lips move, nearer. Before he meets my lips, he angles his jaw and softly kisses the crown of my head, I pause in reverie. He's always sweet with his gestures, but I suspect I have salad breath, and that's the real reason for not kissing me on the lips.

Ever conscious about my smell, I dip my chin down. Instead of pulling back, he lowers his lips to rest by my cheek and whispers, "I think we should get married."

I stare forward as heat engulfs my face. We talked about marriage. Some. Like in passing. Casually. Someday. He knows why I want to get married, but we never talked about a timeline—or anything happening anytime soon.

I turn to look at him, seeing the seriousness on his face. "Sorry, if this isn't the most romantic. I think by now you know I'm sort of impulsive."

I shiver. Maybe it's goosebumps. I'm stunned by whatever is going on. "So, that was an accident?"

"No." He pins his somber gaze on me, a faint echo of his smile lingers there. "Not an accident. Just interesting timing. It's been on my mind a lot lately. I guess it just tumbled out. I know you had wanted to get a teaching job and all that first, but you're subbing. It's practically the same thing. What are your thoughts?"

"Of course I want to get married." I place my hand over my heart as it seems to be pounding harder by the minute. I never planned on Jackson. I honestly believed I wasn't worthy of a man who loves me and Bella as much as he does. I didn't think those types of men actually existed. Now that I've found him, I definitely don't want to risk this slipping through my fingers, but I've always wanted to take things slow, for me and for Bella. "I-I," I stutter with the knee-jerk reaction to try to come up with a reason we can't get married now. There's really nothing. No red flags. Bella adores him. Honestly, it's my heart's biggest desire. Just thinking about it cracks a smile wide on my face. "I-I think I'm ready too."

The creases by his eyes deepen as his smile inflates. He leans over and presses a kiss to my forehead before whispering, "Just making sure we are on the same page."

Bonus Epilogue

Jackson

Sunday night when Kaci goes to pick up Bella from her dad, I make my own pickup at Jackie's house to grab Rigsby. It's been a while since we've hung out together. Jackie and Tom have settled into a routine with their little family. Baby Royan is no longer a baby, as he's already one and an early walker. He's a lot of fun to be around, if you can keep up with him, but I'm looking forward to spending some time with just Rigsby. It's more than just some funcle time.

Tonight, I have a mission.

Not just any mission.

It's all hands on deck and that includes Frankfurter.

When Rigsby walks out to my car, he proudly steers Frankfurter in a harness and leash. That harness was a nonnegotiable from Jackie when she allowed Rigsby to keep him. It wasn't too hard to break the news to Jackie. She didn't even seem that surprised. I suspect she knew all along but went along with it to see how far Rigsby would go. After all, the ferret lived in his room while he was in school all day. It's absurd to think she never looked in the back of his closet. She did comment that she had found it interesting that over the summer Rigsby had taken a sudden interest in always putting away his clean laundry. She also laughed when she recalled how she noticed a musty odor in his room, but she blamed it on the fact she'd cut down on housekeeping from being sick and pregnant. Boy, was she wrong.

Rigsby scoops up Frankfurter, he opens the door and drops the ferret in first before he plops down and shuts his door. "What's the big secret?" he blurts out, his eyes finding mine in the rearview mirror.

Shifting the car into reverse, I back out slowly. I actually can't wait to tell him. I can't wait to tell anyone. I've been holding this in all day, but of course I'm going to tease him a little. "Well, I can only tell you if you promise to keep it a secret."

"Yeah, of course." He leans as far forward as his seatbelt will let him.

I shift the car into drive. "First, sit back in your seat." I pause, watching in the review mirror to make sure he scoots back. "Now, I need to know that Frankfurter can keep a secret or—"

"He can," he cuts me off. "He lived in my closet for months. He's cool. I promise."

I take an extra long time and rub the scruff on my chin, pretending to mull it over. "Okay." I drop my voice almost to a whisper to make the news even more exciting. "If you promise, I'll tell you."

"I promise!"

"Well, you know Kaci and I have been together for a year, right?" I pause to run my tongue along my bottom lip as everything about what I'm about to explain makes me unnerved in all the best ways.

Like, I can't sleep at night.

I just lie awake, thinking about how I'm the luckiest man in the world. All my dreams are about to come true. Even though I'm not sleeping, I'm not at all exhausted. If anything, I've never felt more at peace with any decision I've ever made. "I'm going to ask Kaci to marry me tonight, but I need you and Bella to help. Oh, and Frankfurter," I tack on as that little ferret actually has the most pertinent role in all of this.

Rigsby's jaw dramatically flops open, and no words come out. I get it. At his age, he thinks girls should have cooties. Marriage isn't exciting for him, but I couldn't do this without him or Bella. They are the reason Kaci and I even got together. In a way, they were our little matchmakers. "So, what do you say?" I ask, one eye on the road and the other on him in the rearview mirror. "Will you help me out?"

His eyes narrow, locking his gaze on mine. "Do I get root beer and wings?"

A chuckle bleeps out of my chest as he's getting to be a good negotiator. "Of course," I say, a mischievous smile blooming on my lips. "Food first and then I'll explain everything to you..."

Back at Kaci's apartment, Bella drags me into her room, "to show me something Little B did," which is our code to get away from Kaci. Kaci just laughs and excuses herself to the bathroom. We have only a few seconds to get organized. I quickly tie my surprise on a string, attach it to the Frankfurter's waist and then hand Frankfurter to Bella with a wink. "Alright, Bella," I say as she takes him into her arms and cradles him like a baby. Even though Frankfurter is Rigsby's pet, he often accompanies us on our visits to Kaci's house, and we've all come to love him and his entertaining antics.

This proposal idea was actually all Bella's. I had asked her earlier this week what she thought about me marrying her mom. She got teary eyed and was excited, but she had one request. She wanted to help with the *asking part*. I thought that was fun. I was thinking about dinner and a quiet proposal at home since Kaci is such a homebody. Bella came up with this idea, and I liked it so much better.

It's a little bit crazy.

But it feels like a full circle moment to me. "So you know what to do. Let Frankfurter out of the bedroom after a couple of minutes. We all pretend to try to catch him, but only let your mom grab him." I cut a glance to Rigsby before I say, "Got it?"

"Got it," they say in unison, both of them pitching back giggles.

Across the hall, the bathroom door opens, and I toss a finger to my lips to silence any talk of our plan before I step out of the room. I align my steps with Kaci's. "Did you want to watch a movie or something?" I casually ask, doing my best to sound bored. "It seems like the kids are playing well for now. I know Rigsby's not going to be ready to go any time soon."

Her gaze wafts to the bedroom door and back to me. "I don't know if I have the attention span to get into a movie right now. Maybe we can just watch some reruns or something that I don't have to pay attention to."

"Sure." I nod, and we walk to the couch, taking our usual spots. She flicks on the TV and places her legs on top of mine as we snuggle into our favorite TV watching position. She flicks through a few of our favorite channels. Nothing catches either of our eyes, and she continues clicking through channels. "Boy," she says after a couple of minutes. "I didn't think it would be this hard. Nothing is on."

"Nope," I agree. "Lately, if it's not hockey or hockey adjacent, I just don't care to watch it either."

"What about the History Channel?" As soon as she switches the channel, the bedroom door flies open, putting my plan into motion.

My heart slams into my chest.

Everything is so real.

I want it to be real.

I've never wanted anything more, but I wasn't prepared for the flood of emotions that would come with knowing my entire world is about to change.

Rigsby screams first, "Frankfurter come back!"

Bella flies out of the room, dragging her feet. "Frankfurter!"

Kaci's gaze whips behind her as the ferret flies by the couch and ducks under the coffee table, not stopping until he leaps on the table, then to the top of the fridge. "Is he scared?" Kaci swivels on the couch, her feet drop to the floor, and she stands.

Everything is going according to plan. She's already headed to the ferret.

"I don't know what happened," Bella goes on like we had re-hearsed. "He has some sort of sore on his belly. I tried to look at it, and he acted like he was hurt and ran away."

"He's hurt?" Kaci frowns as she advances toward the fridge.

"I didn't notice anything earlier, but we better check him out." I stand, pretending to also be concerned but I hang back, allowing her time to grab him.

Both kids run to the fridge, dancing on the tips of their toes as Kaci swipes him from the top. It's actually surprising he doesn't resist more because he usually makes a game out of being caught, but he loves Kaci.

"What in the world?" Kaci's words drift out, confusion laces in her tone. "Bella, did you tie something around him?"

"No." Bella's reply is fast and truthful since it was me who had tied the little ribbon around his belly.

"He has a string wrapped around him." Kaci narrates, her finger tracing the red yarn. "He must have gotten wrapped up in something. No wonder he's upset..." Her voice trails off as her gaze freezes on the yarn, and she gasps.

"What is this?" she asks weakly. I step behind her and place my hand on her low back to steady her *just in case.*

"It's an engagement ring!" Bella blurts out. That wasn't rehearsed at all, but it's cute, and I release a nervous laugh.

Kaci looks at me expectantly. "Is this for real?"

Kaci seems to be stuck in a state of shock as she is just holding the ferret out in front of her. I take Frankfurter from her and pull the string to release the ring into my hand. Then I pass the ferret back to Rigsby, and turn to Kaci, her eyes brimming with tears. I didn't expect to feel my heart in my throat like this. *Phew.* I've thought about this moment so many times—each time I got emotional but that was nothing compared to this.

Taking a deep breath, I adjust the ring, pinching it between my thumb and forefinger. My knees actually weaken, so it's a relief when I drop down on one and hold the ring out to her. With my free hand, I take Bella's hand and pull her next to me.

I swallow, letting my gaze linger on the ring for a moment before I look up to her. All I can manage is a tear-filled rasp, "Kaci, I love you. I don't want to imagine my life without you and Bella. What do you say, will you marry me?"

With tears in her eyes, she takes my hand, squeezing it, and whispers, "Yes."

I don't wait another second to take her into my arms, and we kiss each other as if we both understand what the other needs. My heart overflows with all the love this woman gives me. I know life isn't perfect. If anything, life has been a little crazier since Bella and Kaci came into my life, but I wouldn't want it any other way. Thanks to Kaci and Bella, I'm the luckiest man in the world—even without a lucky glove.

Thank you for reading Come and Get Your Glove. As you may have guessed, Elijah will be getting his own book. That should be coming later this year. Please watch for that. I actually have a lot planned for these guys.

Would you like to get a super-secret peek at what is coming next for Granite Ice?

I'm taking a slight turn, not leaving the series completely, but I wrote a hockey adjacent book because I had so many requests to write Sam Summer's (Sophie's brother's book). It's coming May 2025 (in less than a month!!!!). You can already preorder here: https://www .amazon.com/dp/B0F6F76N1D?ref_=pe_93986420_775043100

Title Reveal!

Also by J.P. Sterling

About J.P. Sterling

J.P. Sterling grew up watching old reruns of Lucille Ball and Mary Tyler Moore and fell in love with wholesome entertainment and slapstick comedy. She loves leaning into the over-the-top humor and full circle moments, especially if it means the underdog gets to shine.

Aside from writing, she's also a wife and homeschooling mom, a holistic dietitian, a former college professor and lover of all-things dark chocolate.

*No swears. Just kisses. No Blasphemies. *

Let's get social!

Hey you amazing reader! You are invited to join my private reader group for all-things clean books and friends. Enter the group here: https://www.facebook.com/groups/happilyeverafterparty

Other places to follow me:

Instagram: https://www.instagram.com/stories/authorjpsterling/

Facebook: https://www.facebook.com/jpsterlingauthor/

Amazon: https://www.amazon.com/stores/author/B01N9TJXJN/about

Acknowledgements

Phew! I made it this far, and I'm as shocked as you are all. If you would have told me I'd be writing sweet hockey romance, I would have laughed so hard, but I've so quickly fallen in love with this team and these guys, and this is not the last book you'll see with Bill Baker and his boys. I have a lot more coming.

Special thanks to my friend and fellow hockey romance author, Kerry Evelyn for walking with me on this hockey romance journey.

I also have to thank my editing team. I added a new editor for this book—Sarah with Perfect Pages. She was great to work with. I also worked with Rebecca again, and she's amazing as always. I also have several proofreaders who helped me out this time: Koren and Valeri. I have a long list of amazing readers I feel like I should type out, but I always forget people and then feel bad, but I want to start randomly calling out a few readers for each book. This is in no particular order as I don't play favorites, but Megan, Peggy,

Tabitha and Debbie—you're shoutouts come first. Thank you for being super readers.

My little family.

All my readers and the entire books community. It's an honor to have a little corner in this space. It really does feel more like an extended family than any "job" I've ever had.

To my writing partner, Brooks. I would have never made it past book one without you.

And to my Father in Heaven, who writes my story better than I ever could.